BEACHSIDE MAFIA

Colleen Ferrary

Colleen Ferrary

Bria Brigante

is not your typical

mafia princess.

He watched Bria control the situation with one simple nod and the words he would learn to dread, "Ricorda il mio cognome," remember my family's name.

Devon would never forget her name.

For Jeannette Ferrary, who has inspired me to follow my dreams and hone my craft. I am so thankful for everything you do to support my dreams.

For my mother, who told me that I could be anything I wanted to be as long as I tried. For my father, for giving me the confidence to believe she was right. For Kathy, who channels her inner Mafioso for me whenever she can. I have been inspired and blessed by you all.

For Aislinn, who has become my muse, my critic and my accomplice. My world moves in your orbit. For Scott, for holding me up when I should be the one holding you. You are both the happily ever after at the end of every story.

I love you all beyond words.

PROLOGUE

"Come with me. Shhh…quiet, Bella Bria."

"Where are we going?"

Her thick Italian accent was hurried and rushed. "Shh. We must leave. No body can know. Come bella. Trust me. Your Papà wants me to take care of you, Bella. I can no do this here. We need to go, Bella."

"Papà is dead." Bria responded in a matter-of-a-fact tone perfected by teenagers.

"Bella, your uncle is dead now, too. We can't keep you safe here. We must go."

"Uncle Sal is dead?" Emotion coming back to her tone. Urgency followed, "Where is Victoria? - Is my aunt dead, too? - What is happening? Why is everyone being killed, Delphina?"

"Bria, there's no time to talk," her nanny hushed. "We must go now, everything is all set. No body can know, Bella. No body."

The car was warm and tucked behind bushes near the staff quarters of her uncle's house. She had been staying there for the past week, since her family was murdered. The lights were all off and a young man dressed in all black stood by the door waiting.

"But my things. My phone," Bria reasoned.

"No phone, Bella. We'll get you a new one. They'll find you. I'll get your things later. A few days, Bella. You trust me, no? Get in the car, bambina. I'll explain in the car. We must go."

Bria slipped into the car in her pajamas. Her nanny's son put a dark blanket over her and hopped in the driver's seat and drove away before her nanny could join them.

"Non aver paura, Bria. Lei sarà con noi presto," the young man said.

Bria's Italian wasn't very good. "Afraid? Where are we going? Everyone is dead. My mother, my father, my sister, and now my uncle. How do I know you're not going to kill me, too? Why isn't Delphina with us?"

"Stay under blanket, Bella Bria. You need safety."

The nanny's son was calm, despite only being slightly older than Bria. What was he doing here? He lived in Italy. Why was he taking her away in the middle of the night?

NINE YEARS LATER

"Julia! Pack your bags! I just purchased two tickets to the Dominican Republic, all-inclusive! Call me! I need to get the fuck out of here for a while and you're coming with me. We're leaving Sunday! Call me!"

Bria slapped down the phone disappointed she couldn't see Julia's face when she heard the news. She ran to her closet. How dare they fire her? How could Brad let that happen?!? Yes, it was a mistake, she thought, but it was her first one ever. She was a major producer for this firm. Clients loved her, she'd dedicated her life to her work. Damn! She was even sleeping with the boss to secure a promotion. That email was only meant for Brad. How did it get distributed? "His admin! I'll get that nosy old bitch!" Bria plotted as she stormed through her closet. She pushed hard, trying desperately to move the overstuffed winter clothes to the side so she could unveil some of her summer dresses. Even though it was only autumn, her summer clothes were already taking refuge in the back caverns of her closet.

With no one to talk to, Bria continued conversing alone. "Tomorrow, I'll look for a new job. Today, I'm treating myself!" Bria talked to herself some more as she grabbed the stack of dresses from the back of her closet and tossed them onto her bed. The sun hadn't even set, and the day had already been so full. This morning started like wheat toast— plain and ordinary. Yet, as the sun set on her Escada sundress that laid atop the massive heap of clothes now strewn across her bed, she realized there was nothing ordinary about this day at all. She had lost a job, a lover, booked a vacation with her bestie, and would now max out another credit card on updating her wardrobe for her trip. "It's late," she thought, clearing her mind. She'd have to limit her retail therapy to Bloomie's. They're always open later. A quick shopping spree and maybe Julia could meet her for a cocktail at *The Meet*.

Bria made a mental list of the things she'd need to complete her beach look. She eyed her Phillip Lim dress in the pile. That would work. The white cotton slip dress with pleated bodice always accentuated her subtle Mediterranean complexion. It made the cut. She'd have to add new sandals and a great hat in order to update last seasons' dresses. She had seen an oversized yellow and raffia Lola Hat at Barney's the other day. She wondered if they would be open. She moved the Jason Wu dress to a second pile that would be shoved back inside the small city closet. She let out a mischievous grin as she eyed the poppy red Cushnie Et Ochs dress. "Hmm…" she murmured, remembering the last time she wore this and the attention it brought. The twisted neckline fell gracefully over one shoulder but dipped dangerously low in the front and back. "This one must come with me."

She talked into the air demanding more items be added to her shopping list "Alexa, create a list. Add a sarong, a new bathing suit, matching beach totes in poppy and marigold…" She paused. Could her credit card bear those sexy new Saint Laurent sunglasses that were just released? "Saint Laurent shades," she dictated to the small black, round speaker that shared the bed stand with her blank journal and her reading lamp. She laughed that her suitcase would hold more value than the entire cost of the trip.

She remembered how her father used to tell her to "Act the part you want, Bella Bria." She was acting the part, all right. As she looked at the pile of clothes on her bed, she realized this was the reason her credit card declined the reservation she tried to make at a nicer resort. Julia wouldn't mind. Bria could be honest with her. She was the only friend she kept from childhood, and the only friend she had had since. She thought about Julia visiting the big empty house in Jersey after her parents died. Only Julia would ever really understand her, because Julia knew Papà, too.

The thought of her father made Bria stop. She stood alone in her room, looking at the elegant journal he had given her a week before his death. When these moments would come in the past, Bria would throw herself into work. There was no escaping her memories today. They surrounded her like small atoms crashing into her skin from every direction.

She remembered her father's giant hands and smothering hugs as she thought about him. How she needed them now. She smiled as she could still hear his booming voice echo through the halls of their New Jersey home when work associates came to visit. Through the door she knew, if Papà was speaking Italian and booming, it was not a good time to enter. His soft quiet voice meant business was good and he could be interrupted. When his voice was soft, Bria would knock lightly on the double doors that led to his massive mahogany desk. Its scrolled, beefy legs seemed an important asset of the enormous desk that became her father's stage. It needed to withstand his enormous fist as it was regularly pounding on it when he held court with his workers.

"It that my Bella Bria?" she'd hear him call, almost as if a different man had interrupted his own conversation.

"Yes, Papà," a then smaller version of Bria would reply.

"Why don't you pour our friends a glass of our special wine, Bella?" She was always so pleased to do so. While she would play hostess, she'd get to overhear some of her father's work talk. This, he would never speak outside of that room. Her father was a shrewd businessman. Often, he'd be visited by mayors and councilmen and business men of varying importance. The thrill of sitting on his lap, knowing her Papà was someone who intimidated them, was Bria's high. She'd sometimes sit on the big staircase and watch visitors pace the foyer waiting for Uncle Louie to call them into Papà's office. When

Bria was invited in to visit Papà, she would place her long dainty fingers on the giant desk and hunch forward, looking at her father's associates. She mimicked him perfectly as her gesture always inspired a revelation and advice from their guests.

"You're just like your Papà, Bella."

"You pay good attention to him, little Bria."

"Your Papà is the master. Are you a master as well, Bria?"

Sometimes she'd hear, "You're a chip off the old block, Bria. You keep helping your Papà and soon this will all be yours. I have a feeling you have it in you."

She had always been "Papà's girl." Only her mother had not been in awe of her similarities to her father.

"Ah! Bria!" her mother would exasperate, "Why oh why do you have to be so much-a like-a your Papà? Always in controlla. Why can't you be a nice-a girl and play with the others?" For a moment, she could hear her mother's thick Italian accent as if she were in the room with her.

Papà had met her mother while on business in Italy. She was working as a model in Milan when they met and fell in love. She followed him home to New York where they started a family. She knew she had been graced with her mother's exotic features and her long, lean legs. But her attitude? That was all Brigante and everyone knew it.

"Act the part you want, Bella Bria." Papà's words snapped her back to reality.

She'd dress for the vacation of a lifetime, she decided. And when she got home, she'd act the part of Vice President of Marketing of one of the most powerful firms in the city. She'd need to, if only to pay her credit card bills that were getting increasingly larger with every dictation to Alexa. She laughed at herself as she checked each balance of her remaining credit cards and memorized them carefully. She sat on the edge of the bed with the journal in her hand. The leather was soft and reminded Bria of the big leather sofa in the family room of her childhood home. It was there, where her fondest memories sat. It was there, that her mother and her sister and her father would sit more on each other than they would on the supple leather sofa. They would pile on top of each other and giggle as they watched movies and looked at photo albums and read books. Now Bria didn't know where that giant sofa was, and she definitely didn't know where her family went.

There were favorites in every family. Bria was Papà's and her sister was her mother's. As the day was getting the best of her, Bria's eyes welled up as she thought of her father. How she missed him. How she wished he was there. "Papà would have fixed everything," she thought. Of course, she missed her mother and her sister as well. But her father? Well, he just made everything OK. Now it was up to her, she was the last Briganti. She would start with an incredible vacation with her best friend to forget this rotten day and push it far from her memory.

Bria checked her cell phone to see if Julia had returned her call. She double-checked her voicemail just in case. Nothing. She had hoped Brad would have left a message saying he had fixed everything. But again? Nothing. She decided to send Julia a text: 'Jules, D.R. in 2 days. Check VM. *The Meet* at 9pm! CAN'T WAIT!!!!'

Julia's response came quick, "crazy rn, cu @ 9."

Julia never turned down *The Meet*. *The Meet* was a trendy new cocktail bar on the East Side. You had to know where it was because the sign was an obscure name plate that looked like a doorbell for the apartments above. After ringing the bell, the door would be opened by the concierge who inspects your wardrobe and asks you,

"With whom would you like an introduction this evening?"

Bria always said, "investment banking," but this evening she knew she would need to schmooze with her own crowd, "Advertising." She answered.

"And your name, madam?"

"Bria Brigante." At that, the concierge paused slightly, as if knowing.

Gathering himself, he continued, "Right this way, Ms. Brigante." The polished host strolled to the back of the bar where vintage advertising posters somehow managed to enhance the industrial lighting fixtures that were carefully wedged between twenty-foot-tall neoclassic columns. Walking into a group of well-heeled twenty-somethings, her host announced, "I think you'll find this group to your liking, Ms. Brigante." He turned to the group and continued, "Allow me to introduce Ms. Bria Brigante. She has a heightened interest in advertising. I'll allow you to schmooze for a bit while I fetch your waiter." At that, the finessed host departed with a warm nod, leaving her standing in the middle of four young junior executives and two senior firm executives. She quickly observed the senior executives moving away from the others. One thing Bria knew how to do was schmooze. She needed to ensure she was included in the right group as they broke apart. The last thing she would do is talk shop. She had to move quickly, or she'd be stuck with the junior executives who were neither intriguing, nor did they hold any promise of career advancement. She noticed the screensaver on one executive's phone as he glanced at an incoming text and said,

"Did you see the match last night against Manchester? Messi choked at the goal. I thought for sure Ronaldinho was going to push Messi into the goal himself. Did you see his expression?"

At that, the two executives jumped at the conversation. The young executives looked at Bria in disbelief as she edged her way between the groups and nonchalantly took over the conversation. Bria smiled to herself as she proudly recalled the highlights from that morning's episode of Sports Center. She had learned to memorize the highlights each morning— and even take notes— so she could recall them later when she needed them. She memorized team flags and colors, knowing she still operated in a man's world and this was the best way to get them talking.

Her second free cocktail, a Brooklyn made with Macallan twenty-five, helped ease the pain of the day. It also reminded her that Julia should have been there two cocktails ago. She excused herself from the small group that had gathered around her, to check on her friend. She walked in the genderless bathroom, checked her appearance in the communal mirror, and tucked herself into an available stall.

No texts. No calls. Bria felt a chill run up her back as her mind considered the worst. Ever since that day, she had always assumed the worst first. She pushed Julia's number on her phone. Her call was pushed to voicemail after the second ring. Well, she's alive, she deduced. She texted: "You OK? Schmoozefest is waiting." Three dots appeared and then vanished. They were back. They disappeared again. This wasn't like Julia. Bria hiked up her skirt and squatted over the toilet while typing the word, "Julia?" into her text field. The three dots reappeared. As Bria washed her hands, she received a text:

"Can't make it tn or to DR. Talk when u get back." She stared at the phone in disbelief. This was not Julia. Was Doug back? Julia was a tall lanky blonde who was continuously mistaken for a model. She had an ease about her when she walked that made the whole world look twice. Even Doug looked twice, before she married him.

Doug was Julia's ex-husband. Doug and Julia were married right after college. Julia was out of his league and Doug knew it, for a while at least. But then the real Doug emerged. Once a nice guy, Doug finally showed himself as a social climber who pivoted like a bobblehead whose magnet was misplaced and caused him to never look straight ahead. This applied to jobs, people, and especially women. Julia was madly in love with him. But Doug? He was focused on who was next. He suffered from hedonic adaptation. In the late nineteen nineties, a British psychologist coined the "hedonic treadmill theory." If you lived in New York City, chances are you have spent some time on the hedonic treadmill. This was the driving force behind many of the high earners and power players. Dr. Eysenck compared the pursuit of happiness for these individuals to walking on a treadmill. Those suffering from this affliction could never appreciate what was right in front of them. In fact, they would have to keep walking simply to stay right where they were in life. Doug was always walking and looking for a better job, better networks, and sadly, a better wife. Bria wished she had never read that article in the *New Yorker*. She wished she had never given this unfaithful and unreliable human being an affliction of which Julia would be compelled to forgive.

"He's sick," Julia would reason each time he begged her to come back.

Frustrated, she marched back to her group and ordered a third Brooklyn with an extra cherry. Bria worked the crowd until she could no longer read the bartender's name badge. She looked at the man with the screensaver and invited him to grab a bite to eat with her. Both executives joined her as they left *The Meet* and headed to a late-night eatery two blocks west.

That would be the last thing Bria remembered until morning.

DEVON

"Fine, Dad! Do that! I don't need your help!" Devon threw his phone toward the couch with the speed of a major league pitcher. He walks across his SoHo loft and poured himself a neat Pappy Van Winkle, a gift from his father when he graduated from Wharton last month.

"Every man needs a good car, a good wife and a great bottle of scotch," the senior Lancaster would preach. The bottle, an AMG GT Convertible, and an introduction to Elizabeth Alexander were delivered to Devon at his graduation party. His father had everything planned, or so he had thought.

"What he hadn't planned was that he would raise a son who had his own mind!" Devon caught himself say the words out loud.

Today's argument was the last of many, Devon convinced himself.

For months, Dylan Lancaster had been badgering his youngest son with his "graduate plan." Devon would join the family business, he would lead the Luxembourg team to start, he would go out on a date with New York's most eligible bachelorette… none of which, Devon had any intention of pursuing. Every conversation ended the same way, with a phone or door slammed and Devon's mother calling him hours later trying to smooth things over. He could hear his father's words:

"Why are you doing things the hard way, Devon?"

It would never be enough, thought Devon. This loft, the car, the allowance, the trust fund… Devon knew, in his father's eyes, he would always be in his debt. That debt would weigh heavily like a noose around Devon's neck until he succumbed to the senior Lancaster's demands. Did Dylan Lancaster even believe Devon could make it on his own? Did he believe in his own son? Devon had tried to get his mother to come around to his way of thinking, but she was weak. She could never stand up to her husband and she wouldn't start now. Every time his father would threaten to cut him off, his mother would magically appear with a check to cover the fees on the loft.

She had no idea that Devon had been investing his allowance and renting out his loft for fifteen hundred a night on AirBNB for the past five years. Most of his renters came from a discreet realtor whose clients came from around the world and wanted to remain unseen during their visit. It was a simple transaction and his loft was perfect for their needs. While at Columbia, Devon would stay at his parent's house or with a friend while he had renters. While working on his MBA at Wharton, the loft was vacant, so he just raked in the money. A swank apartment in SoHo was an easy sell. He hated to think about how many married old geezers had had sex on his bed, but he couldn't deny the profits. He simply paid his housekeeper extra to keep quiet and purchased extra sheets, so he didn't need to think about how sleezy it all was.

The first time Devon's mother handed him a check, she recommended a separate bank account that Devon's father couldn't access. She didn't want to infuriate her husband any more than Devon already had. That was five years ago.

His mother's generosity and Devon's ingenuity and investments now totaled over seven hundred thousand dollars in that secret account. When the senior Lancaster would start directing his future for him, Devon would be tempted to write the old man a check just to shut him up. Just thinking about the shock of doing so, gave Devon great pleasure. But, as things would have it, he would always talk himself out of it.

"You need money to make money," so the saying goes.

His father's voice would ring in his head, "It's money and timing that builds wealth, Devon."

He knew there was truth to that, but there was something else you needed: balls. This is what Devon had but his older brothers lacked. They hadn't stood up to Dylan Lancaster. They took the scotch, the car and the girl and they never looked back. Devon was different. Whom he needed to prove that to more —himself or his father— was uncertain. What Devon did know was, he needed a break from New York and the pressures of his family.

He decided to buy a ticket to Tortola and get some much-needed rest while he planned his next move. Besides, going off the grid would infuriate his father.

He called Max.

Max Bloomfield III was the heir to the most revered tropical resorts around the globe. He knew Max was planning to winter in Tortola on one of his properties there, perhaps it was time for a visit?

Unlike Devon, Max had no other desires than to work for his father. Considering Max was constantly surrounded by beautiful people in bikinis— or less— Devon could understand his friend's choice. This winter Max would be, as he called it, "hanging poolside learning the business in Tortola." Max was smart, but far more of a playboy and trust fund kid than a plutocrat. What did come naturally for Max was the ability to be in the right place at the right time. At Wharton, Max could find every party involving someone you wanted to know or needed to know, and then he could get you invited to it. Mark Zuckerburg was being entertained by the Wharton administration the evening before finals.

"What's going to serve you more, a meaningful conversation with Zuckerburg or a good grade on your Advanced Business Analytics exam?" Max would goad.

He was right, the night was invaluable. Before five o'clock, a dinner invitation came for Max and one guest to not only join the evening's events, but to sit at the Facebook giant's table for dinner.

Devon dug his phone out of the Danish Panton-inspired cloverleaf sofa that sat as a conversation piece in the center of his trendy loft. Its thirty-four-thousand-dollar price tag seemed worth the value when he thought of how great a party could play out around its curving clovers. With seating that forced you to look intimately at the person next to you, it turned out not to be as comfortable when you were watching a football game as it was when you were thinking about romance. He sat on the back side of the sofa looking out toward the bustling street below while the phone connected.

"Max? Devon. I'm on my way."

Devon knew, if he left now, he would be truly on his own. Could he really do this without the help of Dylan Lancaster?

BRIA'S MEN

Bria's head begged for mercy. Damn! Where was she? She looked to her left to find the man with the screensaver naked in the bed next to her. Shit, how did she do this again? She looked around for her clothes which didn't seem to make their way into the bedroom. She slipped out of the bed quietly and grabbed the Brioni button-down that was tossed over the butler. She quietly shut the door behind her as she tried to recall the evening's events and crept into the kitchen. There were no walks of shame for Bria. She'd walk out proudly, grab a cup of coffee, and make herself at home in this unknown destination. As she gently clicked the bedroom door shut behind her, a voice greeted her from the kitchen.

"Good morning, Bria. Last night was amazing. You're a fucking wildcat." The other executive stood behind the counter embracing a freshly brewed cup of coffee. He lifted the glass Chemex toward her, "Ready for a cup? It's still hot."

She froze. What had she done? Her first ménage a trois and she couldn't even remember it? This was an all-time low, even for her.

"I'd love some." She refused to indulge him with fake accolades, especially ones she couldn't recall.

She rounded the counter to see her companion sporting nothing but a partially hard penis. "Down, tiger. Not before coffee." Bria knew how to play it cool. She knew how to stay in control, that is, until she didn't, which usually involved drinking. The door behind her opened and Screensaver gave her a crooked smile,

"I wondered where my shirt went."

Woody, or at least that's what she would call him because of his slightly erect penis, chimed in, "It looks a hell of a lot better on her."

The three sat barely clothed at the counter and drank coffee. The man with the screensaver rubbed his head and said he needed to get to work. He told Bria and Woody to help themselves to eggs or yogurt and walked back to his room to shower. As the shower started, Woody stepped behind the sandstone island and pulled out some eggs.

"Over easy?"

Bria wondered if he intended the pun. "Sure."

She got back to her apartment around noon. She checked her messages, nothing from Julia or Brad. She picked up the itinerary she had printed out for her and Julia. If Julia couldn't go, who could she invite? Brad? She was so angry with him still. He just stood there quietly yesterday as she packed her things and was escorted out. No, definitely not Brad. She had a lot of female acquaintances, but no friends. She was too busy focusing on her career for friends, she told herself. She decided to call her cousin. She hadn't talked to Victoria since the funeral. Her call was denied after the third ring and went to voicemail. "Vic, it's Bria. I happen to have an all-inclusive ticket to the Dominican Republic tomorrow and my friend just had to back out. Do you want to join me? It will be like old times. I miss you. Ciao bella! Call me."

Sadness cloaked the small apartment. Bria knew Victoria would never respond. For some reason, Victoria and her mother blamed Bria for her uncle's death. He died in an accident, only days after she had moved in with them. She was seventeen. She was sent to live with a nanny days later, where she was home schooled until she went to college. During that time, Bria had little touch with the outside world, not that she wanted any. Even Julia had disappeared during that time. When she received a full scholarship to Wharton for marketing, that would be the last she heard from her nanny, or anyone else from the family.

It was then that she reconnected with Julia through Instagram. Bria's nanny had convinced her to create a new online name, Brianna Bell, in honor of her father. Julia was eager to reconnect but explained how she had tried to find her online after she had left her uncle's house.

"It was as though you were gone, too." Julia had said.

She had been unable to find any trace of Bria. Her aunt and cousin had been equally uncooperative. The pair had finally been reunited. Until now, Bria would have thought Julia and she would never be apart again. She dialed Julia's number. Julia's phone was turned off and went straight to voicemail.

"I guess I'm on my own." She pulled herself up like a prize fighter. She had just got knocked on the ground. She was now in the corner ready to get back in the ring and defeat her opponent. Going for the win was what Bria Brigante did best.

Bria carefully organized her clothes in her massive suitcase. She grabbed her travel tote and stashed her wallet, passport and six hundred dollars in cash inside before heading to the shower. As the water pivoted off her shoulders in the small stall, she lost herself in yesterday's events. The email that she sent Brad— rather, the email that was sent to everyone— it was provocative. They were lovers. Of course, the fact that he was married figured very little into Bria's thinking. It made it easier. "Besides, He started it," she would rationalize. She just didn't say no. She originally thought she could use their relationship to her advantage. Then the relationship became fun, dangerously fun. She found the rush of breaking the rules intoxicating. She tried to not think of the other life Brad was living, but instead, she relished the benefits this kind of relationship held for her.

Brad was the CEO of Vicci Marketing. He was her boss. Vicci was an up and coming agency that catered to Italian clients who wanted to build their business in the States. Innumerable fashion houses, car manufacturers and vineyards relied on Vicci to sell their product. Bria was the best they had. Her model mother, notable Italian heritage, and fearless confidence worked together to make her a driving force in the Vicci business model.

She should have been the Executive Vice President of Operations of Vicci.

She was pacing to be.

She had even said so in her email to Brad. She detailed the ineptness and ballessness of the current EVP. She questioned if *he* would sleep with Louis Camilleri of Ferrari if he wouldn't keep Marchionne's commitments to Vicci. She knew she would. Bria Brigante would do whatever it took to win. The email then went into great detail as to how Brad knew—from firsthand experience—how skilled she was in that particular line of persuasion.

That damn admin, she thought again. Why wouldn't Brad step up and say it was a joke? Of course, it was a joke. She tried to convince herself that it was a joke, but she knew it wasn't. Nothing would keep her from getting what she wanted. That was the Brigante way.

She wrapped herself in her mother's silk robe after her shower and embraced a fresh corretto. She still had a couple bottles of her father's grappa that she used to make it. Each time Bria would make a corretto, she'd remember the way her mother would lovingly make the espresso. She replicated the ritual as she moved across the room to choose one of the thin necked, hand-blown, glass bottles of grappa. She used it sparingly, hoping her supply never ran dry. She gently stirred in the grappa with the small silver spoon. Her mother always delivered these to Papà personally. As she'd place the corretto on the table next to him each night, Bria would watch as Papà would touch the side of her mother's face with his giant hand and whisper, "Ti amo."

"Ti amo," Bria said as she raised her cup to the air. She held the treasured drink as she got lost in the nostalgia. She stared out of the small apartment window to the street below, missing her family more than she ever had. Loneliness was not a family trait. When her parents were alive, so was her home. Dinners were filled with cousins and uncles and friends. Dinner out with their immediate family meant dozens of visitors stopping at their table to squeeze her cheek and pay respect to her parents. It was a rare occasion for it to be only the four of them, but when it was, Papà always made it special.

That was gone.

Bria tried desperately to hold on to the memories of her family. As she stared out at the streets, she remembered the trips to the city with her father. They had both loved New York. She remembered going to Ferraro's Bakery and eating linguine and clam sauce on Mulberry Street. He always had someone else drive, so he could sit in the back with Bria. It was almost always Uncle Louie. As she stared out her window, her nostalgia got the best of her. A dark, familiar face seemed to be gazing back up at her from the street. She wiped her eyes which had now been flooded with tears. Did she know him?

Loneliness had always been her enemy, and now, now it was making her see things.

TRIPPING ALONE

As predicted, Victoria never returned Bria's call. Bria grabbed her bags and headed out of her apartment. As she looked back, she saw her mother's silk robe hanging from the bedroom door and the wine decanter that once sat on a bar cart in her father's office. The photo albums that her nanny had carefully crafted looked like a series of law books sitting next to her father's wine decanter. Despite all the clutter, she had purposefully left that shelf clutter-free. She relished the pictures in the albums, but the wine decanter represented everything she wanted. She wanted a family. She wanted a successful business. She wanted to feel love again. She wanted to feel like she had then when the decanter was full, and she would be in charge of emptying it. The decanter would stand alone, Bria decided, until it was filled once again with wine and shared with family. Until then, it would remain alone on the shelf, like Bria herself, she thought.

She laughed thinking that the dowry she inherited from her mother made her modern city apartment look like the cramped cluttered quarters of an old Italian grandmother. She didn't care. Until her home was full of people, it would be full of memories. She looked at the old aluminum espresso pot sitting on the apartment-sized gas range. Her mother's favorite plates sat piled above on a shelf. They were thin, pottered plates and bowls, hand-painted with Mediterranean blue and delicate yellow designs. She looked at the hand-blown venetian glass that sat artistically on a lace scarf, undoubtedly tatted by her great-grandmother. The collection of artifacts made her feel at home, but as she walked out to the Lyft she had called, she knew she was very far from it.

Devon's driver pulled to the front of the JetBlue terminal and popped the trunk of the Town car. As he signed the paperwork for the driver and added a tip, he was reminded that his father's car service had refused to pick him up. Devon knew he could spend money quickly and he needed to be more economical if he were to prove Dylan Lancaster wrong. He didn't need his father. Although, he took his mother's check this morning, without any hesitation.

She had come to see him off and handed him a check for twenty-five thousand dollars.

"This should get you through until your father comes to his senses, darling. I'm worried, Devon, this time it might take a little longer. I've never seen your father so angry. Why don't you take a nice vacation and think about working at the office after you're refreshed a bit? Maybe just for a little while, darling?" This was her form of a lecture. It was more of a plea. His mother said this as she put the folded check into his hand. Perhaps it was really a bribe?

"How will you explain this to Dylan, Mother?" asked Devon while ignoring her plea.

"I have my ways, honey. Don't you worry. You just go rest with your friend Max. Your secret is safe with me. It will do the old goat some good to worry a little."

At that, his mother grabbed both sides of his face and drew him down to her for a kiss. "Thank you, Mother." Devon offered.

"I love you, Devon. Have fun and call me when you arrive." His mother waved to him as he disappeared into the town car. Devon thought about her standing with her driver in front of his loft until he was out of site. It was a surprise to see her, but he was thankful. She also just bought him two months of not having to dig into his savings.

Devon decided to belly up at the airport bar and start his

vacation early. He approached the bar next to a twenty-something woman who was clearly accustomed to finer things. As he pulled the bar stool out, he noticed her long lean legs seemed to reach for miles. She barely glanced at him as her long dark hair draped in waves over one shoulder. The other shoulder stood proudly alone, accentuating her sensual frame and illuminating her perfect olive skin. She carried herself like a movie star, he thought. Confidence raged from her as she chatted a banker-type sitting to her right. Devon couldn't decide if he loved her or loathed her at that moment.

"How could he love her?" He laughed at himself. He had just laid eyes on her and she had barely given him a second look.

"A Brooklyn, please? Chilled, with Macallan." She was graceful in her tone. The bartender had no idea what a "Brooklyn" was but was clearly eager to please. He seemed helplessly awash in admiration for his newest patron. Devon wondered if the bartender had any idea that she was completely out of his league. As the bartender moved around the corner, Devon watched him type something into his phone, presumably searching for the ingredients for a Brooklyn. Devon leaned forward toward the bartender,

"While you're pouring the Macallan, I'll take mine neat. Do you have twenty-five?"

"I'm sorry, sir, twenty-five?"

At that, Devon remembered his newly absent allowance. "Never mind, whatever Macallan you have is fine." Devon needed a new drink to go with his new budget.

The dark beauty flashed him a crooked smile. Had he got her attention with his drink order? Devon immediately loathed her. A gold digger, he surmised.

Devon grabbed his drink and moved across the bar, finding a small table with two leather chairs. He could not only see the departure board, but he could watch the poor sap at the bar get eaten alive by this beautiful barracuda. As he enjoyed his whiskey, he noticed he wasn't the only one watching the show. Next to him, sat a middle-aged man with a gold ring. The ring sat on his pinky, pinching his skin to hint of a once younger, more svelte, man. The only thing more noticeable was the matching gold chain around his neck. Devon thought of the heft of the necklace, and then of the ring, and then perused the remaining clues of this man's existence. His St. Louis baseball cap was a stark contradiction to his leather jacket and chunky gold accessories. He looked at his shoes. Ferragamo driving shoes. Not Ferragamo's best, but good. The shoes, Devon thought, may be the only part of the ensemble he would consider wearing. His father's voice echoed in his head,

"Devon, there are some things you just can't buy. Taste is one of them."

Devon started to think of all the remaining things money couldn't buy. He sipped his Macallan and continued watching the seductress at the bar. His mind ricocheted from one paternal lesson to the next when he noticed the man with the pinky ring pick up his phone, his eyes still locked on the temptress.

"Yeah, I'm with her. She looks just like her mother... Yeah... No, I got her."

Devon couldn't help but overhear his conversation. His voice was deep, gruff. Devon looked toward the bathroom, then the surrounding tables. He couldn't remember seeing a woman with this unusual man. The man with the pinky ring was becoming more of a mystery than the vixen at the bar. Devon toyed with the idea of starting a conversation with the man but decided instead on a second Macallan.

PRE-PLANE ROULETTE

There were few things that would keep Bria's mind off her current situation. The first was whiskey, the second was free whiskey. Scoring free cocktails was child's play, especially for a savvy marketing exec like herself. She knew how to present and promote product, and in her game of "bar bingo," as Julia had named it, she was the master. Her mind kept wandering back to Julia. Whether Doug stepped back into her life or not, she wasn't that girl who would turn her back on a friend in a time of need.

Bria walked into the airport bar preoccupied. She knew she was dressed to kill and decided to sit next to a broker. His Stefano Ricci crocodile loafers were what grabbed her attention first. But it was his Patek Philippe Nautilus, that ensured he was a hedge fund guy. The fortieth anniversary edition was hard to come by and a sign of success in Manhattan. The hedge fund set seemed to buy them all. A flashy extravagance to let the world know you've made it. Papà had had a love affair with watches. Bria remembered his associates giving him the newest and greatest watches in return for his favor. Despite his vast and growing collection, his favorite was his Yacht-Master Rolex. He had received the Rolex from Bria's grandfather, when he gave Papà the business. She couldn't help but wonder for a moment, "What had happened to his business?"

Bria sat at the bar next to the broker, her art of seduction stuck in auto-pilot.

"That is quite a timepiece! My father would have loved that watch," she waxed poetically to the stranger. "He collected Patek Philippe and Rolex but this one seems different, more powerful in some way... Please tell me about it?"

The stranger obliged.

"Oh! The fortieth edition?" Bria feigned, "Even with all my father's success, this sounds slightly out of his league." He corrected her slight ignorance and impressed her with the price tag,

"Yes, the fortieth edition is almost three times the price of a standard Patek," he boasted.

She knew she needed to show strength, elitism, but a dash of vulnerability with his type. "And I imagine they must be impossible to get?" Bria masterfully worked her victim as the bartender approached.

Her gentleman, careful to raise his bejeweled wrist, motioned the bartender, "Please, get this stunning woman a cocktail, please."

"A Brooklyn, please? Chilled, with Macallan."

She turned back to her bingo game with the broker when she heard, "While you're pouring the Macallan, I'll take mine neat. Do you have twenty-five?"

She was distracted by the previously unnoticed man to her left, the one ordering Macallan twenty-five. She looked to her left and was surprised to find a young, athletically built, light-haired man standing next to her at the bar. He couldn't have been more than twenty-four but ordered an accomplished man's drink. She couldn't help but assess him. "Hm...when had he arrived?" she thought. She couldn't help but now notice his strong chiseled chin and piercing blue eyes. She shot him a half smile and quickly brought her attention back to her broker. The game should not be lost over a chiseled chin, she scolded herself. She felt the twenty-four-year-old move away from the bar. Happy that her distraction had left, she continued learning all about her latest pawn's successes. As he droned on, Bria's mind skipped from Brad to her parents to Julia to her job as if they were having a raucous game of tag on the inside of her skull.

Two Brooklyn's later, Bria excused herself from the bar to head toward her gate. The broker handed her his card, which she would quickly discard on the way to Gate E15. Nothing beat flying first class, but this trip would be anything but.

She sat with the herd of vacationers on one of the hundreds of blue, plastic, curved seats. Bria stood out sorely from the young families with vinyl sneakers and flashing-soled children. The innumerable groups of college students filled the waiting area. Watching them pass cash around as reimbursement to each other, it was clear to Bria that they lacked the willpower to wait for the free drinks that would be included at their budget-friendly, all-inclusive resorts.

Across from Bria sat an elegantly dressed woman in her eighties with a large straw hat. She sported strong red lipstick and what appeared to be expensive plastic baubles in orange and island blue around her neck, perfectly matching her floral pants. As she clutched her small carry-on on her lap, she couldn't help but wonder why this woman would be alone on a flight to the Dominican Republic. Bria shared in the woman's loneliness for a moment. She and the woman with the baubles were traveling alone to a tropical island.

Redirecting her emotion, she looked away. To her right, several men with Ralph Lauren polos and busy cell phones stood, furiously wrapping up business. They'd escape New York for a few days. Bria pictured them gathering at a resort where they'd do nothing all weekend but golf, drink, smoke cigars, and flirt with women they had no intention of entertaining. It would be all about the ability to hook them. It was the classic game of married fishing. One of the married men would cast their bait across the bar, maybe even send over a cheap, showy cocktail. The unsuspecting woman would accept it, flattered, and make her way over to his table to thank him. The release always seemed to happen in one of two ways with these groups. One man would work to reel in his mermaid, feeling pretty good about himself. Inevitably, this desperate vixen will sit on his lap or slightly too close as his loyal friend decides it's time to have some fun. A phone comes out, pretending to take a picture of the "cute couple," and the man jumps up with the fury of a rich man without a pre-nup. The poor girl doesn't know what has happened and she's patted on the ass and given a going away cocktail as the men go back to their revelry. Occasionally, a more morally bankrupt group will bring the girls to their room. In those cases, the pat on the ass comes sometime before breakfast.

Bria couldn't help playing this game as she travelled. She'd scan the room and ask herself, "Who are they?" She'd then make up an entertaining story of their sordid past and tawdry present. She was sure her stories were far more fabulous than the boring lives most people lived. Thinking of someone else kept her mind active and away from the pain that always chased her.

She opened her newly acquired Sonia Rykiel leather tote and grabbed the hand bound leather journal her father had given her the week before the accident. She opened the cover and looked at the note he had written on the first page:

Bella Bria –
Non permettere a nessuno di cambiarti interiormente,
ma impara da chiunque tu incontri.
Mia cara e bellissima Bria, lascia che queste pagine siano un posto in cui conservare ciò che hai imparato dalle nostre lezioni in modo possano proteggerti e guidarti in futuro.
Ti voglio bene Bella Bria.
Papà

She read the words over and over. "lascia che queste pagine siano un posto in cui conservare ciò che hai imparato dalle nostre lezioni in modo possano proteggerti e guidarti in futuro. Let these pages be a place to keep what you have learned from our lessons so they can protect you and guide you in the future."

Her family was killed only days after Papà gave this to Bria.

For the first time, Bria wondered if her father had had a journal. Where were their things? After moving to the city with her nanny, she couldn't recall what happened to their home, their furniture, her mother's jewelry... Yes, Bria had a small apartment filled with treasures, but they had had so much more. Everything happened so quickly. She would have to call Victoria's mother when she returned.

Bria looked at the blank pages on the journal with sadness. "I've learned so much, Papà" she thought quietly. "I'm sorry I didn't listen." Her emotion started to overtake her. Just as she was about to flip through the blank pages in the journal, she heard the static of the speaker above her head announce the boarding of her flight. She resolved to write one lesson she had learned in her journal before the end of her flight.

The plane was crowded and smelled of sweat, beer, and Axe cologne. She was thrilled to think there would be an extra seat next to her— Julia's seat— so she could have some space between the beer breath and her perfectly coifed hair. She took the window seat in her row and stuffed her Sonia Rykiel in the overhead. The seats were small, and her long legs touched the seat in front of her. As the captain announced they'd be pulling out in four minutes, the flight attendant stood at the end of her aisle. A father who sat in the aisle seat, and whose screaming children sat with his wife in the seats across the aisle, rose suddenly. He pushed his heavy legs into the seat in front of him as he straightened his body upwards in an awkward angle to the floor. Recognizing this lazy attempt to clear a path was not going to be successful, the flight attendant gracefully asked the man to remove his body from the row entirely. At that, she waved another passenger toward the empty seat next to Bria.

"No, I'm sorry," Bria abrupted. "I've bought both seats. This seat is to remain empty." The husband looked at Bria with a look of disdain followed quickly by relief and admiration. It was as if he knew his wife had planned on tossing a screaming kid across the aisle at him, and now, he had a perfectly good reason why she could not.

"I'm sorry, ma'am, but we're not showing this passenger has checked in and our flight is overbooked. I'll be sure you get a credit." As she was about to contest, the old woman with the expensive beads arrived at her side. Bria looked at the woman and, realizing the battle was lost, welcomed the beaded woman into her empty seat.

"Thank you," said the flight attendant smugly. She knew Bria's type. She also knew that even the most callous bitch could not resist this eighty-year-old woman with floral pants and matching baubles. She sashayed as she walked forward in the cabin, infuriating Bria. It was time for the pompous flight attendant to start telling people who would not even pretend to listen, how to save their own lives during an emergency landing.

Bria, along with everyone but the delightfully polite octogenarian next to her, looked away from the emergency presentation. She again opened her leather journal. She would need a scotch for this part, she thought. She then looked at her two companions and knew bar bingo would not be in the cards on this trip.

"Hold my hand, darling," said the frail, baubled woman.

She obliged.

"I'm still a little nervous since my Donny left me. I've never enjoyed flying since the angels took him." Bria enjoyed the cool of her soft, bony hand as it touched hers. She placed her other hand over the woman's and smiled.

"Was Donny your lover?" Bria asked seriously, while trying to keep it light.

"You might say," the sweet woman replied, "Let's talk after we're in the air. I'm too nervous right now." Bria could feel the woman's hand shake. The plane lifted off while Bria smiled and comforted her new friend. As the plane leveled out, the woman reported, "Oh, I thought I would feel much better. I'm still as nervous as a June bride."

"Why, I think you might need a cocktail to calm those nerves. They'll be around soon," Bria giggled. The old woman looked up at her with wide, light-blue eyes. They were framed with soft wrinkled skin that gently overlapped and held traces of hair that once formed eye brows,

"Oh, but I'm on a budget now that my Donny has left me."

The flight attendant pushed the cart to their row and Bria handed her credit card to her, "A Bloody Mary with Tito's, please, and whatever my new friend would like." The old woman didn't skip a beat,

"Might you have Macallan's darling?"

Bria stopped breathing.

"Why yes, we do. I have eighteen here but could come back in a moment with the twenty-five if you'd prefer. I'll need to get it from the first-class cabin."

"Oh, that would be lovely," said the old woman. She glanced at Bria, "I'm sure this will do the trick my dear. Thank you. My Donny would be so grateful to you."

Bria couldn't help but smile. She had been had. She knew what she would write on the first page of the leather journal. Using her best Italian, she wrote:

Anche il truffatore può essere ingannato.

"Even the bullshitter can be bullshitted," was what she really wanted to write, but her limited Italian would not allow it. This seemed more eloquent. She smiled out the window to the clouds flying under the plane. She had just been bested at Bar Bingo.

Bria had no idea an even bigger lesson was left to be learned on this trip.

VINNY

His leather coat was sticking to his beefy frame. He swore under his breath about the coat, about the heat, about the impromptu trip he had to take. He peeled his coat off as he noticed the wet stains that marked the silk lining. Vinny grumbled and swore a little more as he tried to take inventory of the damage. He had wished he had time to pack. Sometime jobs required flexibility, and he was finding this one did. His took off his St. Louis Cardinal cap and ran his fingers through his damp hair. Being in the back of the plane made disembarking in a tropical island miserable. When the doors opened, and the metal stairs rolled up to them, Vinny could feel the rush of heat pour in. Parents with car seats and drunken college kids clogged the aisles while Vinny stayed focus on his charge. He watched out the window as she cat walked across the tarmac. Every eye turned. That was the problem with Bria Brigante, he thought, every eye turned. Between that and her lack of predictability, she was like chasing a cat. She'll be caught when she wants to be caught, he thought.

All he needed to do was get close enough to find out where she was going. Once he had that, it would be cake. He could go buy some clothes and take his time. One thing he had learned thus far is, Bria Brigante wouldn't be far from the bar.

He stood at the luggage corral with his ears focused behind him. "Ocean Caribe, Punta Cana," he heard her tell the cab driver.

TORTOLA AND BIKINIS

"Devon! Over here!"

Devon stood in the center of the lobby with its tall arches and gleaming marble floors. A white grand piano commanded the lobby while the grand chandelier and enormous potted palms in their immovable Caribbean blue urns brought the outside in. As Devon was handed a cool damp towel, he searched the lobby for Max's voice. There was no telling where the inside ended, and the outside began. Devon searched for a wall but could only find one at the top of the massive curved staircases where they gracefully met at the top. As Devon followed the voice, the sun seamed to glow from a patio where it hailed strongest. He looked past shorter potted ferns in the same, strong ceramic urns. He noticed outside, past the urns, gold wedges of fabric were hung tightly over elegantly appointed tables. They looked like small sails, keeping the sun from the diners and creating a tropical garden where the temperature was perfect. As Devon made his way toward Max, the breeze tickled his nose with the aphrodisiacal air. Max rose from his seat as he wiped his last bite from his lips.

"I'm sorry, my friend, I didn't expect you until later." Max gestured to the empty seat between him and his father and invited Devon to sit.

"Devon, it's great to see you, young man. How's ole' Dylan doing? It's been years since we've seen your parents." Devon should have expected Max's father to ask about the infamous

Dylan Lancaster. How should he answer? Their fathers had been golf buddies back in New Jersey for most of Devon's childhood. Although they had owned some of the world's best resorts, Max Bloomfield II could not stay away from the fast pace of Manhattan and Fairmount Country Club.

"This is where the real business happens, boys," their fathers would say.

Max and Devon lost touch through boarding school and undergrad years but were reunited at Wharton. Max Bloomfield II and Dylan Lancaster stayed close until the senior Bloomfield decided to buy a yacht and skip summers up north. Rumor was, there was a business deal that went wrong, but neither Max nor Devon could pry it out of their parents. Devon wondered if this meant the truth would be OK to share.

"He's well, Mr. Bloomfield. Some stories never change." Devon decided to only answer the question and leave out the detail.

"And your brothers, Devon. How are they?" Max Bloomfield II wondered.

"Still kissing father's ass at the firm." Said Devon dryly.

Both Max's chortled. Mrs. Bloomfield feigned indignity.

"Well I'll tell you, Devon. You've always been my favorite. What are your plans now?"

Devon glowered. "Well, Mr. Bloomfield," Devon started.

"It's Max, now, son. You're a grown man, call me Max."

"Well, OK... Max, that's what I'm here trying to figure out."

Now Max Bloomfield II glowered. "Well I'll tell you what, son. You and Max get caught up this week and I'll be back Monday. Why don't you and I meet up on Monday and I'll see if I can't help you out a little bit. It would be an honor to be of help to an old friend."

Devon knew this meant that Max Bloomfield II would enjoy one-upping his old friend Dylan Lancaster by being the one to help his youngest son.

"That would be great, sir." Devon smiled. Devon didn't know if this would be great or not. Devon knew that's what he should say, but he knew Max Bloomfield II was no keener on the idea than his father, of his not following in father's footsteps. He might as well enjoy the week, he thought, before having to meet with his father's adversary and defending his decision.

Mrs. Bloomfield had the staff bring Devon a bevy of local delicacies and small bites while the three men caught up. No one could possibly eat all the food the staff would deliver but he was thankful for their generosity. He was more eager to get to the pool and see what Max really enjoyed about his father's business.

Max and Devon were finally able to escape the necessary trappings of the afternoon and head to the pool. The resort was filled with beautiful people, an extraordinary amount of skin, and a complete absence of fat.

"Ahhh…. Now I understand," teased Devon.

Devon looked at the luxurious cabanas that lined the pool of the hotel on one side. On the other, a long bar with teak shutters peeked out of the water. It was there where vacationers enjoyed sleek cocktails while sitting on submerged stools in the crystal-clear water. As you looked past the bar, the long pool seemed to fall off a cliff into the sea and palm trees flanked its breathtaking view. Max, dressed in a hotel polo and white shorts, invited his friend to "Dive right in!"

"No, no, Max. I'm here to see you!" Devon lied.

At that, both men laughed heartily. As they laughed and caught up on the few months since they had seen each other last, Max finally took a serious tone.

"So, buddy, what ARE you going to do? You still saving up your stash?" Devon nodded to acknowledge the money and stared into the pool.

Finally, at almost a whisper, he said, "I don't know. I want to prove Dylan Lancaster wrong, but I'm not sure how. I wish something would just jump in front of me and say, "Hey stupid, over here!" but it doesn't. At least it hasn't." Both men were quiet for a while.

Finally, Max offered, "Dude, maybe you can help us out for a while here? We're having a problem with a couple of our resorts, I've looked over the books and marketing a million times, I just don't see it. You have a pretty good eye for that if I remember correctly."

Devon protested, "You don't have to pay me to do that! Whatever you need, I'm here. I'd be honored to help."

"Well, let's enjoy your week first. Let's have some fun and maybe we'll get you a job as a bartender, so you can hide out from your father. Who knows, maybe the thing you're looking for will swim up to the bar? Hehehe." The men laughed.

"To mermaids!" Max toasted again.

"Here's to my new career in espionage!" Devon laughed while meeting Max's glass.

Devon never imagined he'd find far more than a crooked accountant.

OLD HABITS

Bria got out of the taxi at the entrance of the Caribe Resort. The cab driver took her suitcases out of the trunk and set them on the side of the car. Bria handed him a ten-dollar bill and looked for the bell hop. At the entrance was a small, round, wooden table. On the table, eight clear plastic cups sat on a rectangular tray lined up like soldiers greeting each new guest. The melted ice rested toward the top of the orange drink while a straw pierced with two cherries and an orange slice leaned to the side in each cup. Next to the tray was a small sign that said, "Welcome to Caribe Resort, please go to front desk."

"The welcome reception?" Bria laughed at herself. If her father could see her now. Julia, she thought, would make this cheap escape funny. How she wished she was there.

Bria grabbed her suitcases and lugged one at a time up the two steps to the lobby. The heat embraced her, almost overwhelmed her, as she rolled both cases to the reception desk.

"I'm checking in. Bria Brigante." Bria stated, eager to get in her room and out of her travel clothes. She looked around at the tired hotel. A group of college students had just rolled out of a van and were surrounding the welcome table. The receptionist welcomed Bria and asked for identification. The receptionist paused. She looked at Bria's dress, at her watch, then her bag and her hat. Bria knew the look of envy.

The receptionist asked, "Is the other party joining you later?" Bria's shoulders slumped.

She lifted them quickly and stated as proudly as she could,

"No, there's been a change. She will not be joining me."

The receptionist handed her an envelope with a key card and the room number written in blue pen on the outside. The key sleeve looked old and worn but Bria eagerly took it. Bria looked around and was about to ask for someone to bring her bags to the room when the receptionist stated,

"If you stay on the path to the left, it will be a little longer to your room, but the trip will be easier with two suitcases."

Bria looked down at her suitcases. She was tired from the trip and the Bloody Mary's. The novelty of the old woman with the beads wore off after learning that her "beloved Donny" was her dead Maltese. Unabashedly, the woman had no qualms in suggesting "maybe just one more cocktail" to calm her nerves.

She was exhausted. She wanted to change out of today and into some fun. She wanted to forget about the huge bar tab in the air, the plastic cups with melted cocktails, and the rundown hotel. She wanted to shake off this week, this year, and this decade.

Bria took the receptionist's advice and dragged her suitcases down the path to her garden terrace. The garden terrace, which online seemed so beautiful, was resort-speak for "as far from the beach and the pool as one could possibly sleep." After a ten-minute walk with her heels twisting on each stone and the bump-bump-bump of the suitcases on the cobblestone, she arrived at room one forty-five. Relieved, she slipped the card key down into the lock. The red light on the lock blinked. Bria took the key and tried several more times, only for the same response. She wiped the magnetic strip on her dress and tried again. Nothing. The idea of dragging her suitcases back to the lobby was overwhelming. She looked for a housekeeper, a gardener, or anyone with a blue Caribe Resort camp shirt on. There was no one. Bria couldn't bear to drag the suitcases back. At this moment, her solitude was again piercing what was left of her being.

She grabbed her leather tote and put her shoes inside. She walked around to the back door of the cottage and tried the patio door. Locked. She went back to the front and pulled her two suitcases to the patio where she carefully tucked them behind a tree. There they would have to sit until she returned. Her feet already throbbed. She pulled up her hair into a simple ponytail to find relief from the heat and made her way back to the reception desk— one painful cobblestone at a time. She returned to the lobby to find the van full of party-goers were now waiting in line for the single check-in clerk. Bria tried to jump ahead, but the group was as drunk as they were obnoxious. She looked at the welcome table. Empty cups and pieces of fruit were strewn carelessly back on the tray giving the impression that the neat little soldiers that previously occupied it had just been hit with a bomb. She could really use even a bad drink right now.

Thirty minutes later, Bria emerged from the lobby with a new key. As she walked carefully back to the cottage, she began to regret her decision to leave her luggage there. The sweat formed between her breasts and she could feel her dress clinging to the small of her back. She hoped that if someone were to steal her luggage, they only had the ability to take one, leaving at least one swim suit. The walk seemed painfully long, despite the lack of luggage this time. Hers feet throbbed, yet she couldn't help but worry about her bags. As she finally rounded the corner to her cottage, she held her breath until seeing a handle peeking out above the hedges. She knew her risk had paid off this time; but tried to recall her father's wisdom on the matter. She'd write it in her journal when it came to her, she thought.

The grounds were pretty in a natural, island way. It was the first time she had slowed her mind enough to notice. There was a natural beauty to the pathway and the flowers seemed to bloom everywhere she looked. She saw a small pond with flamingos and later came upon a peahen in a small grassy nook. The peahen was large and brown and stood stoically in the small grassy nook, proudly donning her emerald feather necklace. Ordinarily, this stunning array of feathers around her neck would garner attention but knowing the grand peacock, with his long train and extravagant plume of feathers may be nearby, left the bird relatively unnoticed. Bria recalled her mother telling her about the peahen.

"You know-ah Bria, the pea hen. She makes-ah all of the decisions. The boy bird, he fluffs out his feathers and does his dance, si? But it's the woman who really makes-ah the decision. You no forgetta. Capisci? Bella? You don't-a have to be the peacock. You are the peahen, Bella. You don't need to do the dance. You are the one that is in charge." Bria didn't feel like the one in charge right now as tears came to her eyes as she thought of her mother.

She breathed a heavy breath and could swear she could smell the beach in the distance. She slipped the newly activated key card into the lock. The red light flashed twice. Bria felt her Italian temper flare. She inserted it again and was relieved to hear a gentle click and be rewarded with a green light. As she opened the door, musty air replaced the Caribbean mist she had imagined. She looked at the two full beds and could only laugh at the polyester floral coverlets and bamboo headboards. "Well, luxury is not what I bought. I guess I'll have to find that elsewhere," she said out loud.

Bria took a clean sheet from the shelf of the closet and laid it over one of the beds. She slowly emptied her things from her suitcase and decided where she would put them. As she filled each drawer and the entire closet, she smiled with relief at not having to fight Julia for closet space. Neither, she knew from experience, was a light packer.

She grew sadder as the pathetic room seemed to close in on her. The beige walls and musty smell overwhelmed her. There was only one cure for that, she thought. She grabbed her favorite new bikini, a cover up, and sandals and headed to the water.

Another ten-minute walk and Bria was sweltering as she followed simple signs pointing in the direction of the pool. As she emerged from the walkway, she could hear the splashing of the water. A volleyball game and games of chicken filled the pool from front to back. She found an empty chair on the outskirts of the lounge area where she disposed of her accoutrement. It was time to head toward the cool water and wash off the trip with a nice, tropical drink at the swim-up bar.

As Bria walked to the deep end, a local vendor stopped her, "Braids, Ma'am? I do nice braids, cheap. Ten minutes."

"Not now, gracias," she polited and walked past to the pool edge.

"You like beads? I have the nicest beads on the beach. You come back, lady. I braid your hair." The woman was now standing next to her.

"No, thank you." Bria said firmly. Bria dove into the pool to escape the annoying vendor and swam up to the bar. The water was warmer than it should have been, she thought. She still welcomed it. Several of the young men looked her way—as well as many of the women. She found her way to an empty stool. The bartender scurried over,

"Mamajuana?"

"Pardon me?" Bria wasn't sure what he had said. Was he propositioning her?

The bartender repeated, "Do you want some mamajuana? It's a specialty of the island. It makes you feel reeeeal good."

"What's in it?" she asked.

"Oh, lots of good things. There's honey and rum, a little wine, and the good ones have some tree bark. Trust me, it keeps the devil away but the men in the mood," the bartender almost sang his answer.

"Well, who can resist that?" Bria showed him her room key and welcomed the native drink.

Two hours later, she still sat at the swim up bar. She had a crowd of men surrounding her now and a larger herd of women scowling in her direction. There was barely a foot between each patron and the water surrounding her felt dirty. She wondered if she looked from above if the bar area would be encompassed in a yellow haze. As her stomach turned at the thought, she knew it was time to go.

Bria emerged from the pool, surprised by her unsteadiness.

"Food," she thought. She staggered through the sea of lounge chairs. She was too buzzed to speak to the vendors surrounding her without stumbling, so she plowed through ignoring their pleas. She sat with a thump on the lounge chair, where her belongings awaited. She clumsily slipped her sandals and coverup on while she got her bearings. Her head moved from side-to-side looking for the all-day buffet she read about. One hundred steps away, she saw a large thatched hut with scores of vacationers waiting in line. She steadied herself and made her way toward the crowd. Her head spun from the mamajuana.

At the buffet, a line surrounded a plethora of fresh fruit and old hamburgers, French fries and a salad bar. Bria needed food now. Alone at the end stood a man with a tall chef's hat in front of two burners. There was no line. Whatever he was serving would have to do. She ambled toward the man when someone jumped in front of her.

"Bolognese," he ordered.

She raised a hand and signaled for the same thing, "Make that, two." The words were harder to form. "What was in that drink?" she wondered out loud.

The man in front of her turned, "Mamajuana, I take it?" Bria nodded. "Yeah, it got us all. The stuff is potent." She nodded again. "You OK?" the man asked.

"I'm OKAAAYY," she slurred in response.

"Hey, I've been there. Go grab a seat and I'll bring this over when it's done." Bria gave him a relieved smile and followed his orders.

The bolognese was remarkably good and she shoveled bite after bite into her mouth. The young man had delivered a small plate of rolls as well "to soak up the mamajuana." She had never been so thankful. She ate the pasta in five minutes but sat at the table for close to an hour. She needed to sober up, she thought. Her lounge chair was only one hundred feet away. She contemplated making a go at it; a little nap would do her good. She hadn't even been to the beach yet, but knew she had no chance of navigating the uneven sand. Bria slowly stood, bracing herself with the back of her chair. "One hundred feet," she said to herself.

Bria made her way to the lounge chair, tripping over two others along the way. She barely felt the resin of the first chair dig into her calf. Her chair was so far to the outside edge of the pool area it was now covered in shade. She landed on the chair and laid back even less gracefully.

As her blurred vision started to move the ground beneath her, Bria took her towel and covered her eyes. She needed to sleep off this potent elixir.

WHERE?

"Ocean Caribe!" Vinny repeated as if saying it louder would make the driver give him a better answer.

"No, no Ocean Caribe, señor," the taxi driver pleaded. Vinny's presence was commanding. The driver was nervous and picked up his phone. Vinny heard him ask the person on the other end if he knew of a place called Ocean Caribe. Vinny opened his phone while in the cab, the "No service" icon was displayed at the top left of his screen.

"God-damn it!"

The driver and Vinny both made the sign of the cross as if begging the Lord for forgiveness for the words that launched from Vinny's anger. The looked at each other. Vinny nodded. After a few seconds the driver said in careful English,

"I'm sorry, sir. I not do know of any hotel named Ocean Caribe. Can I to bring you another hotel?"

Vinny thought for a minute. "Bring me to the best hotel in Punta Cana."

He had been following her since the host at *The Meet* called him. Bria Brigante had expensive taste. She must still have her father's money, he thought. After witnessing her bevy of Bloomingdales' and Barneys' bags, he was sure he would find her at one of the better resorts.

Vinny had no idea how close he was.

SWIMMING NAKED

Bria woke with a start. She sat up from the lounge chair to find an empty cement field between her and the pool. The pool was now decorated with floating displays of gaudiness. Four plastic floral arrangements were highlighted by a battery-powered luminary stuck in its center. They floated carelessly and gathered at one end of the pool. The swim up bar looked long abandoned and the plastic lounge chairs were stacked neatly along the edges of the patio. At the far end, a pool boy hosed away the day's debauchery.

Bria tried to imagine the time and looked toward the thatched dining hutch. It was packed with tourists. It must be seven or eight, she thought. Her head throbbed as she lifted it. "Hair of the dog," she thought, careful not to remind herself of the mamajuana that sent her into such a deep slumber. She wrapped her sarong around her waist and decided to grab a cold beer and walk on the beach before going back to her room to clean up.

As she left the stench of the Caribe Resort, the palm trees led her to what she was really looking forward to enjoying; cool, clear, Caribbean waters and soft white sand between her toes. She lifted her newly opened can of Presidente to her lips. There was something tawdry about drinking beer from a can on this beautiful beach. It was free and Bria's head desperately needed it. She turned to look for landmarks of her new home for the next seven days and noticed vendors moving her way. "No, no gracias," she held up her hand to ward off the vendors. "No tengo dinero!" Her tone was firm and demanding. That stopped the troupe dead in their tracks. Bria turned, proud of herself. She imagined she probably seemed believable in her hungover state. But it was true, she thought to herself, *no tengo dinero*.

Bria's walk was regenerative. Bria's thoughts shifted from her lack of money to the vendors'. How could they survive on the pittance they were asking? Their sales techniques warded off half of their potential buyers. Even worse, much of what she had seen was underpriced and could be sold at four times the price in the right venue. She watched the children of the vendors. They didn't beg, although their appearance might dictate they should. The vendors were proud. They were doing the best they could. Perhaps she would start braiding hair and teach them some better techniques. She smiled thinking that, maybe, they could teach her to braid hair!

The moon seems to light up the entire sea. It seemed close enough to crash into the earth but seemed to dance magically on the water's horizon. Its mirrored light bounced off the waves and illuminated the beauty of the miles of gentle ripples. This was the best Bria had felt in days, which wasn't saying much. She had been deadening her senses with alcohol since she was escorted out of Vicci. Bria walked barefoot on the edge of the water, allowing the foam to caress her feet. The almost empty Presidente dangled next to her thigh as she walked. She should think of turning around but kept walking anyway. It had become the norm to override her own instincts. It was quiet, and peaceful here, minus the occasional vendor. Most vendors congregated by the beach bars at this time of night, where the population was greater.

After a long stretch of uninhabited beachfront, Bria approached a row of shanties that disrupted the sandy oasis. They were painted in bright island colors of red and yellow and blue. Painted on the first of them, were the words "Hair Brading" with a missing "i." She thought of the annoying woman at the pool. She wondered if she should feel sorry for her rather than be annoyed by her. Was she at a bar right now trying to find hair to braid? Was she home, taking her meager income and trying to feed a multitude? Did they work around the clock? Bria was consumed with the lives lived by these Dominicans. She looked at the makeshift market. Each shanty was a different color and now, abandoned for the day. The shanties leaned into each other as though a strong wind might blow them over. A young boy, maybe eight or nine, sat near the last hut. He sat directly on the sand with only worn khaki shorts and bare feet. His feet looked hardened from the sand as he sat with his soles facing out. He surrounded a stone and two sticks he appeared to be carving. As Bria watched the boy, he watched her. They didn't speak or acknowledge each other, they just stared. Suddenly, the boy's gaze shifted.

"You should watch out for sharks," a man said in a thick Italian accent behind her. Bria was caught off guard. She hadn't heard that accent in years. Startled, she composed herself and retorted,

"Land sharks? I can handle myself with them, thank you." She looked at the man walking next to her.

His hands jumped up as if to protect himself from being hit by Bria, "No, no, no! Your leg; there's so much blood. You might be bleeding to death."

Bria glanced beneath the lazy Presidente to find her calf covered in dried blood. She made a funny noise and then said, "I had no idea." She stopped and investigated the source of the blood and stepped slightly closer to the surf. The gouge on her leg was more of a thick scrape and two inches long, but the blood covered her calf. She took a handful of water and winced with pain as she washed off the blood with the salted sea.

"Now, you are calling the sharks to visit us," the stranger commented. "Are you OK, Bella?" She couldn't help but pause, "Bella." It had been almost nine years since she had been called "Bella." Her eyes instantly teared. "No, no, no… no crying, Bella. I will help you." Bria was infuriated by his assumption of her weakness and looked at the stranger for the first time.

The man wore no shirt, but his dark brown hair covered his shoulders in amazing waves. Around his waist, he had a long, fringed linen scarf that partially covered his casual shorts. He was barefoot, and his well-defined chest and abs reminded Bria of the Italian surfers at La Spiaggia. The beach there at La Spiaggia was filled with rich playboys. Sardinia was where the real surfers went. The man standing next to her was confident, and sexy as hell, but reeked of a womanizing playboy.

"How did you cut your leg, Bella?" he asked sweetly.

"I'm not sure, perhaps at my hotel?" She and the stranger walked and talked. He told her how he was disowned from his domineering family in Italy and was told to take a part in the family business or take three hundred thousand euros and leave.

"You left your family? And you have been surviving on three-hundred thousand euros?" Bria asked in disbelief. She didn't tell the stranger how her family had left her, she just let him continue.

"Ah, Bella. I have not even touched the money. I live off the interest from the three hundred thousand euros!" he said, puffing his chest. He shared stories of how the interest from the money affords him comfortable housing on many islands around the world. He just came from Fiji and Bali. This year he had decided to visit the Caribbean.

Bria couldn't imagine how this was possible, but he assured her he hasn't worked in five years. He told her how he rented an apartment on the island for less than fifty American dollars a month and the woman who owns it feeds him dinner if he takes out the garbage.

"You Americans! The natives see you coming. They charge you triple for everything."

"I think maybe your landlord enjoys seeing you walk around with no shirt on," Bria reasoned.

"Perhaps, my Bella." Her comment gave him permission to unleash his real desires. "Bella, swim with me."

He had fallen a few steps behind as he removed his pants. Bria went to remark about sharks as she found a beautiful stranger completely naked running into the surf. With the water up to his knees, he faced his new friend tempting her to join him. She couldn't help but admire the entire package. Pretending to be embarrassed by his public nudity, she looked away.

"You're crazy!" she shouted and turned abruptly to head back to her hotel.

"No, no Bella! There are no sharks, only me. Bella, join me!" he shouted from the water. Bria marched past him and headed toward her hotel. She sensed him dive into the water as she walked away and thought about how fun it would have been to join him. But she couldn't. She wondered why her moral compass was kicking in at this moment.

"Wait, wait, Bella!"

She looked back to find her stranger naked and chasing after her, his clothes in his hand. She had never seen a naked man run and was amused by how his generous penis moved like a pendulum as it slapped one leg and then the other. She turned away, embarrassed by where her eyes had gone.

"Bella," he shouted again. Bria walked closer to the resorts, away from the sea, for fear her stranger might be more than just carefree and lustful. As she passed the Blooming Sands Resort, she recognized its name from travel magazines. She made a note to visit there tomorrow. Her stranger continued chasing her, naked, and calling to her. An older couple sat on a luxurious settee on the beach in front of Blooming Sands, watching. As she stepped closer, she noticed the expression of disgust and concern that filled their faces. What a scene, she thought. She looked back at her stranger as he noticed the same. He stopped abruptly and stood, facing the older couple. He moved his arm of clothing behind his back, looked at the couple with his nakedness on full display, and bowed as if acknowledging the queen.

"I do hope my wife and I have not disturbed you? I do wish you a fulfilling evening signore, signora." Bria couldn't help but smile. She walked toward him finally, and then, toward her hotel.

Bria made no apologies for the cheap hotel. She walked down the path to her cottage as the long-haired god followed. She wondered when he had put his pants back on. His scarf now hung around his neck, damp from his hair, and she noticed his strong physique in the hotel light. The stranger took the key from her hand and opened the door. He led her into her own room as if it was his own. He grabbed her forcefully once they entered the room and turned her toward the wall, pushing her against it and raised her body from the floor. He moved her lips toward his. The pressure of his muscular build suspended her from the tiled floor, and excited her more. She wanted to beg for him to devour her, but she didn't need to. He was completely in control. Bria may have been sober, but she was drunk with lust. Watching this beautiful man in the water, running toward her, chasing her, bowing naked in front of the offended couple, and apologizing for he and his wife's behavior... it didn't scare her. It excited her. His lack of modesty and confidence made Bria want this man even more. He didn't need gold to be rich, she thought. His lean, muscular biceps easily lifted her weight. He kissed her passionately, forcefully. She could feel his pelvis against her. She could feel him throbbing beneath her sarong. Her bare stomach was flattened against his abs and she longed for him to remove her bathing suit.

The stranger lifted her passionately, never removing his hungry lips from hers, and moved her to the bed with the sheet. He removed his scarf and tied her hands above her, and then to the bamboo post. Nervousness shot through her body. Ecstasy soon replaced it. He moved his tongue over her body until she couldn't manage her emotion any longer, "I need you!" Bria screamed, as if begging for mercy. "Please..." she begged.

But Bria was not in control. The stranger was.

BLOOMING SANDS RESORT, TORTOLA

"Today will be a day for sightseeing," he told his butler.

"You'll need better shoes if you're going to leave the resort. Some of the terrain is rugged," the butler suggested. .

Devon smiled. "Juan, I don't intend to even as much as leave the pool."

Juan smiled knowingly and then suggested darker sunglasses, so the husbands wouldn't get angry. Devon smiled at his butler's foresight and thanked him for his help.

There was something about having butler service in your suite that changed your experience. Having your clothes unpacked before finishing lunch was nice, but Juan had also stacked the bar with several fine scotches, organic vodka, and most of Devon's favorite snacks. When Devon had asked Juan if he knew how to make a Brooklyn with Macallan, Juan apologized but was back in minutes with cherries, bitters, and simple syrup. He had a Brooklyn perfectly mixed before Devon finished rinsing off. His father would be horrified that anyone would dilute fine whiskey—even an ice cube was a sacrilege. He could imagine how appalled he would be with a Brooklyn. It was delicious, he thought—even more delicious knowing it would infuriate Dylan Lancaster.

At the pool, Devon laid on the plush lounge chair sporting his darkest sunglasses. When Devon made plans to stay with Max, he had no intention of staying there for free and would never have expected butler service. He would thank his good friend for his overwhelming generosity when Max returned to the pool to have lunch later.

He couldn't focus on the beautiful people or his lush surroundings or even the warm sun touching his skin. Devon's head was in one place. He couldn't think of anything but what was next. He has been asking himself the same question for the past three years. He wished his father could understand. Devon remembered Pops, his grandfather, telling him about his father.

"He was so stubborn," he'd say. "Devon, your father could have been set for life. I was going to give him his first apartment complex. All he had to do was parlay that into more. You know, son, that parcel was such a great investment that your father would have barely needed to work." His grandfather always told the same story when the family was all together. But it wasn't how his father snubbed his nose at his grandfather that moved Devon, it was how the story ended. It always ended with Pops patting Dylan Lancaster on the shoulder saying "But what does an old man like me, know? I thought I was helping you. I would have been holding you back. I'm proud of you, son."

This was the piece that infuriated Devon the most about his father. How could he not see Devon's need to try to make things happen on his own? This only made whatever path Devon chose to take next more important. He couldn't be wrong.

"You slimy bastard!" Max called. "Have you been sitting here all morning ogling women? Have you not even budged from this seat?"

Devon replied slyly, "The sites here in Tortola are beautiful. You might even say, gorgeous."

Max laughed. "Don't I know it. I don't want to work for my father any more than you do… but the perks here are undeniable." Devon knew this was a lie. Max didn't want to work. Max would do enough to show that he was adding value so his father would give him space to enjoy the perks of his position. That was the core of Max's ambition.

At that, the waiter interrupted. "Mr. Lancaster, might I get you another Bloody Mary, sir?"

"Not now, thank you," replied Devon.

"Let's get out of the sun and have a bite to eat. I might have a proposition for you," said Max.

The two friends ordered lunch on the elaborate patio, this time, without Max's parents. It took Max less than a minute to get down to business. Devon couldn't shake the thought that Max was about to get Devon to do his dirty work, and he wasn't wrong.

"Dev, remember yesterday I was telling you about the three Blooming Sands locations that are underperforming?"

"Of course."

"Well, my father has hired consultants to review the resorts and make suggestions. I think these cases are different. Each property is run with the same standards we have everywhere else. We are either missing something incredibly obvious or someone is stealing money from us. If it is theft, the three are suffering the same way so it must be someone high up in our organization. They'll know about the audits next month and I'm afraid, well, our timing to investigate theft might pass. Devon, we're talking about millions of dollars being lost."

"So how do I fit into the solution, Max?"

"Well, I talked to my father about putting someone in undercover. The problem is, we need whomever that is to be a financial wizard as well as a good spy. I want you to do it."

"Me? I'm not a spy." Devon denounced. Devon's face contorted with a sour smirk and a wrinkled brow. If ever Devon displayed his last name on his face it was at that moment. Clearly insulted by his friend's suggestion, Max was quick to respond.

"I don't need you lurking around the property sneaking into rooms! I need someone who knows how to make friends and get people's trust quickly. I need someone who can ask the right questions and read between the lines. It also needs to be someone I trust. You fit the description." Max explained.

"You forgot to mention my penchant for financial wizardry." Devon goaded.

"Oh yes, Devon, and you are a financial wizard." Max agreed, as if placating his friend to convince him of the task.

Devon knew Max was worried he couldn't solve the problem on his own and Devon's visit was perfect timing. Maybe focusing on something besides himself and his future would be good for Devon.

The two spent the remainder of lunch talking about the problem and alternate solutions. Max opened some of his books and Devon joked about the butler not being so free after all. Devon asked questions, and Max sent messengers for more papers and books. Both Max and Devon had open laptops and soon their table in the dining room was surrounded by the dinner crowd.

"Let's move this up to my suite," Max suggested and then apologized. "I'm sorry, Dev, I know you're on vacation."

"Are you kidding? This is what friends are for, Max. I'll help you in any way I can, but this... this does seem a little crazy. I see a correlation between the islands' economic downturn, but it makes no sense. This generally will make an upscale resort more profitable as expenses lower and the world economy continues to grow. And still, even if it did correlate, that would only account for a million a year, tops. And why is the effect happening six months after the economic downturn? All three have solid food sales but are taking a bath in liquor sales and reservations." Devon was speaking mostly to himself.

"Yes, both areas which can be easily skimmed with cash receipts because of the lack of supervision."

"That's a lot of cash. I'm not sure how that goes unnoticed by your in-house security teams. Unless they're in on it?"

"Exactly. This is my opportunity to prove MY father wrong," Max noted. To this, Devon could connect.

"OK, Max. You win. I'll leave tomorrow. Which location first?"

"No Dev. Enjoy the week, then go," Max insisted.

"Hey, I'd rather have something more exciting to talk about with your father than my future, next Monday. I'll leave in the morning." Devon was firm.

"Okay, how do we sneak you in there? Perhaps as a VIP? The senior staff will be all over you," Max asked, knowing any other option he suggested would be an insult.

"Well, I know how to make a Brooklyn." Devon replied.

MISTAKES

Bria awoke the next morning. Her arms and legs were exhausted from the night before. She could still feel the stranger between her legs, but he was gone. He must have crept out in the middle of the night. Bria writhed in bed, reliving the amazing sex she had just had. She moved her hands over her own body. Even her exhausted body couldn't help but respond to the thought of this stranger. She had never had sex like this. She tried to remember his name. Did she know it? She looked around the room for a note or a calling card. Nothing. Nothing! Bria jumped out of bed. The reality of the situation hitting her.

She had let a stranger into her room, he snuck out, she knew nothing about him, how could she be so stupid? Thoughts raced through her mind. She ran to her closet and looked at the room safe. It was open slightly and Bria inhaled deeply. How could she have done something so foolish?

She knew nothing about this man.

Bria stepped out of the shower, still breathing heavily from her earlier scare. No, he didn't steal from her, but what did she know about him? She used no protection. How stupid. She was completely lost in the moment. Great sex is no excuse for stupidity. She knew she was spinning out of control. This is not the life her family would have wanted for her. She looked at her leather-bound journal, "I'm so sorry, Papà."

Bria decided to go for a run and clear her head of the toxins she had been drinking for the past several days. She threw on a sports bikini and stashed thirty-eight dollars in the hidden pocket in the bra. She grabbed her journal, a towel, and her slides and walked to the beach where she would claim a good spot before they were overtaken by the rest of the guests. As she walked by the pool, yesterday's bartender waved at her.

"Mamajuana?"

Bria smiled and said, "Never again! But keep the vodka cold, I'll be back after my run!" The receptionist from check-in stood next to the bartender.

"How far do you run? The beach makes it challenging, no?"

Bria was proud, "Well, I'm thinking five miles, I usually run ten." The employees wished her well and reminded her to stop and drink water, so she stayed hydrated with the island sun.

Bria smiled and headed toward the beach.

She could never imagine how this run would change her life.

Bria ran furiously, berating her body for her mistakes of the past week. She thought about passing out on the lounge chair, cutting her leg, and sleeping with the stranger. Her anger pushed her legs forward as she thought about the week before she left. She was betrayed by Brad, lost her job because of some idiot secretary who didn't mind her own business, slept with — apparently— two men, maxed out her last credit cards on clothes for this trip, and Julia... what the hell happened to Julia? Her anger pushed her legs across the soft sand mercilessly as they pleaded for her to stop. The burning hurt. She liked it. She liked hard sex and pushing herself until it hurt. It lessoned other pains. Her legs screamed for mercy as she continued to pound the sand with her bare feet. Occasionally a small stone would remind her that she wasn't paying attention. "It would be different after this trip," Bria coached herself as she ran. After her run, she'd rinse in the cool sea, and then join the leather-bound journal by the pool. "No alcohol when I return," she promised herself. Her legs still felt heavy from last night's exploits. No, no alcohol. She would write in the journal, she would plan her future, she would...

Bria kept pounding on. She had long past the old shanties

and had outrun dozens of pesky beach vendors.

"You need sometin' to relax, lady?" they'd yell.

"No run, shop lady!"

"I make a good deal, I go back to your hotel wit' you to get da' money so you take wit' you!"

"Run by my pictures, lady. Nice paintings here, lady." The vendors' voices became a buzz in the background. She drowned them out with her determination.

"I am the vice president of the best advertising agency in Manhattan. I am strong, I am healthy, I don't need a drink to ease my pain." With each step she talked herself into a better future, a better life, a life her father would have wanted for her. She returned past the shanties and this time didn't hear their voices at all. She'd write in the journal. She would be the daughter Papà would smile on from heaven. Bria's legs were crying in pain. She'd better be careful that she cooled down before going into the ocean. Her muscles could seize and she'd be in trouble, she thought. Her right leg hurt more than the left. She stared down at her calf to see her wound reopened and recoloring her calf. She wouldn't stop. She thought about sharks and the stranger again. Her anger at the stranger, her anger at herself, it all propelled her forward. She was coming close to her hotel, she'd slow now and rinse her calf before she got near many tourists. Again, the sting of the salt water made her jolt.

"The pain reminds you that you're alive," she remembered and continued rinsing.

Her father had said that when he came home with a gunshot wound. He told the family he was mugged and shared the unbelievable story of how he got away, beating the mugger to a pulp. Uncle Louie, who was driving, was quick to add more graphic images for everyone.

Bria limped slowly toward the hotel beach. Her leg stung but had stopped bleeding. She touched her bra to ensure the small amount of cash she had secured there was still safe before she jumped in the water.

The water was an incredible reward for her body. She wondered if she had enough on her credit cards to splurge for a spa day. She'd check the balances when she got back to her room. It would be worth the splurge. She'd have one more paycheck waiting when she got home to cover her for a bit. Finding a job should be easy— she was a force in her field. Her portfolio alone would be one other agencies would pay dearly to acquire.

Bria waved to the bartender as she returned to her lounge chair.

"Mamajuana?" he yelled.

"Not right now," she yelled across the pool.

He insisted, "No, no. The bar is not too much fun without you. Come, my lady."

"I'm going to rest for a bit, here. Maybe later." Bria shot him a million-dollar smile and made her way to the chair. She opened her journal and took out her pen and wrote her second lesson, "Pain reminds you that you're alive."

Bria sat staring at the book for close to an hour. "Papà, why can't I remember your face any longer?" Her heart was aching. This always happened when she was alone. She could go months working sixteen-hour days and not seeing the light of day. The minute she stopped, memories came flooding in and broke her heart. Even worse, they made her furious. Anger was a dangerous emotion for Bria. Anger was what provoked self-destruction and her take-no-prisoners attitude. Anger fueled the email that got her fired and thousands of other mistakes Bria had made.

Bria stood up.

"I'll make your mamajuana now?"

Bria started to walk toward the pool but remembered the yellow urine haze in the water. She politely waved and decided to go back to her room and change before visiting the bar at Blooming Sands. Maybe just one drink, she thought.

Bria walked the long path, proud that she resisted the urge to day drink. She looked to both sides of the path cautiously. Was the peahen still there? If there was a peahen, there must be a peacock. Perhaps she could find it? It always surprised her how the male peacock was the more dramatic of the peafowl. The same applied to ducks. She thought of the stranger again. He was definitely a peacock. She giggled to herself as she entered her room. It smelled different. The musty smell was replaced by— what was it— cologne? Bria's brain raced for answers as her eyes scanned the room. Could it have been the stranger's? No. He smelled of sand, and salt, and wine. Maybe the housekeeper's perfume? The door leading to the small patio was ajar. Bria stopped.

Could it be the smell of someone who was still there?

Bria noticed the dresser drawers slightly opened. A bra strap stuck out of one drawer and a pair of shorts were wedged in the bottom closure. Someone had gone through her drawers! Was he or she still there? Bria ran back to the door and looked outside for someone to help her. There was no one. She thought about the self-defense classes Julia had dragged her to. The instructor was hot, and Julia and Bria kept going until finally he asked Bria out on a date. She was prepared.

"Open the bathroom door, Bria," she said in her head. "You've got this." Bria remembered her sexcapades with her instructor. She had more fun not having sex with him than having sex. They played a game— if he could get to her— he could have her. It was weeks before Bria "let him win." She was unnaturally good. Papà had a Jiu jitsu instructor come to their home to give him private lessons for as long as she could recall. Bria loved to take lessons with Papà. He even had Gucci make a gi for her for their weekly lessons. She could do this, she again convinced herself.

Bria took her stance and kicked the bathroom door in. She postured herself in case someone came flying out. When the door hit the tile wall, she heard a loud crack. The door bounced forward to almost closed. Bria used her again-bloodied leg to push it open with less force. No one was there.

Bria kicked the beds to find solid platforms beneath them. The curtain that blew slightly from the open door was her next target. Nothing. Bria exhaled. "Thank God," she thought.

She looked around at the room and started doing inventory. Her clothes were all there. She went to the closet. Still full. She looked at the tiny safe on the shelf. It remained open like it was this morning. Did she leave it open? The blood rushed from her face. She was sure she had closed it. She moved her hand slowly to the safe, already knowing what she would see. She was right. She saw nothing. No cash. No credit cards. No phone.

And worse? No ID. Bria's passport and drivers license were also gone.

THE HUNT

Vinny walked up to the front desk with a hundred-dollar bill folded under a picture of Brianna Brigante. A small edge of the bill showed, as he held the picture up to employees of the Blooming Sands Resort. The picture was aged and wrinkled but it was all he had. He thought of pulling up a picture of her mother. He was sure it looked more like her than the photo.

Although his leather jacket had been replaced by a Tommy Bahama button-down and a straw fedora, Vinny's Ferragamo black leather driving loafers and bulky gold pinky ring seemed oddly out of place to everyone but Vinny. The salesgirl tried to convince him to buy canvas loafers, but they didn't have his size. The last thing he wanted to do was go to another store; too much was at risk. He needed to find the girl and take care of business. There was no time for shopping sprees.

After asking his sixth employee, a large man wearing a shirt labeled "SECURITY" approached Vinny in the lobby.

"Can I help you find someone, sir?" the security guard asked.

"Yes, I'm looking for my daughter. I haven't seen her for years and I want to bring her home."

Puzzled, the guard asked, "How long has it been?"

"Nine years," Vinny answered. He decided to stay as close to the truth as he could.

"Well, how old is she now, sir?" asked the guard.

"Twenty-six. Twenty-seven?" said Vinny.

"You don't know the age of your daughter?"

"Damn," thought Vinny. He recovered, "Ahh, you'll get older too young man. I forgot, she just had her birthday, she's twenty-seven." The security guard relaxed and looked at the picture. Vinny had deposited the hundred-dollar bill back into his pocket thinking this might make the guard more suspicious.

"No, I haven't seen her," he answered flatly. "Sorry."

Vinny knew not to attract anymore attention. With his upcoming job, he didn't want to be memorable.

PUNTA CANA

Devon stepped off the Bloomfields' private plane. They offered to take him by helicopter to Blooming Sands, but Devon laughed at the idea of the Blooming Sands' newest bartender being personally flown by helicopter to the resort.

"We'll tell them we're transferring you from our Tortola resort and it was our way of thanking you," Max assured him.

"Let's not give anyone anything to think about." Devon assured him that his new plebian lifestyle was only temporary, and he would survive. Now, as Devon stepped into the thirty-year old taxi with no air conditioning, he was rethinking his decision.

Blooming Sands Punta Cana was even more beautiful than the resort in Tortola. This surprised him as Punta Cana had become a cheap destination for spring break and low budget company meetings. The cab clunked through the entrance to the resort. Devon watched as he passed a mile of pristine beach views protected by a tall iron fence that ran for at least a mile. The long driveway teased its guest with quick glimpses of its championship golf course and perfectly lined royal palms. As the cab drew up to the entrance, a fleet of Lincoln Towncars and Suburbans seemed ready to whisk guests wherever necessary. The blue taxi, like the resort, didn't seem to fit. Max had explained that they had invested in the land to build a champion golf course. This was a long-term plan. They knew they would have an opportunity to get a PGA tournament next year and, that alone, would be a game changer. Blooming Sands, Punta Cana would become a destination for world-class golfers.

This was an even more important reason for the resort to be operationally sound as soon as possible. Timing is everything, Devon thought.

The moment the driver stopped, a gloved hand opened the door of the taxi while another motioned for the driver to open the trunk to free Devon's bags.

"No, I travel light," thanked Devon, "I have a backpack and a duffel bag right here." Devon thought to leave his designer luggage behind and traded a Robert Graham button down for an old backpack from the bartender he trained with in Tortola. In it, Devon threw a couple Blooming Sands polos and white shorts that Max had given him.

"Really playing the part," Max noted as he drove him to the airfield. "Thanks, buddy."

Devon introduced himself to the attendant as the new bartender. The attendant's demeanor immediately changed. His English became less careful and his accent grew thicker.

"Welcome, brothah. We'll be sure to be down that way wit you."

"Where do I find human resources?" Devon asked, shaking his new friend's hand.

"Oh, you go tru the lobby and go down da hall on dee right side of the reception desk, brothah." Devon fist-bumped his new relative and followed his direction.

The lobby was similar to Tortola, but the ceilings seemed slightly taller. The non-existent walls were dappled with long sheers that flowed elegantly around each entrance. There were no grand staircases, but the Blooming Sands' signature grand piano stood elegantly center stage. A man in a seersucker suit and a hard, straw hat drew gentle sound from the piano. When the pianist began playing an Oscar Peterson piece that challenged the most sophisticated of jazz pianists— Devon marveled at the sound, as did Blooming Sands' most sophisticated clientele. Devon had to stop and wonder if he was still in the Dominican or if he had stepped on the wrong plane and landed in the French Quarter.

Devon walked down the hall and looked for the door marked human resources. He knocked gently and realized he had never before been in a human resources office. He was greeted by the most congenial woman he had ever met. She was energetic and impossibly positive. She welcomed him as if she had known him for years and then proceeded to share all the wonderful stories Max had made up about him. She told him they had had a scheduling problem and his first shift would have to be this evening. Devon agreed, if for no other reason than to stop her incessant apologies.

"Of course," he assured her, hoping he was working alone so his lack of knowledge might go unnoticed. He would be sure to keep the cheat sheets nearby from his new friend in Tortola. The overly appreciative woman then showed Devon around the hotel and to his quarters.

"Staff doesn't have to share quarters, as other resorts require," the friendly ambassador told him. As she spoke, Devon wasn't sure he had ever seen a room so small. Most of the staff was local, but the resort kept rooms for talent they couldn't find on the island. Devon had once shared first class with several New York Knicks players. He couldn't stop thinking of squeezing them into this tiny cubicle. He laughed at the thought of any of them fitting on the small twin bed that was freshly appointed with white linens and a light duvet. At six-foot-nothing, even Devon's feet were sure to dangle.

Once she left, Devon looked around the room. It had everything he needed, he convinced himself. There was a hot plate and a coffee maker, although he could dine in the kitchen for free. There was a small shower stall and a bathroom where the door could not open inward as there'd be no room for it to swing. Max offered a nicer room, but Devon told him he preferred to go deep under cover. Watch what you ask for, he thought. How he missed his butler, Juan, right now. Devon stood in the center of his new home and spread his arms out to the sides as far as they could reach. He was only a foot away from being able to touch both walls without moving. He laughed at himself.

"Imagine!" he thought. "This is where I could be living if I don't figure out what to do with the rest of my life!" Devon knew he was helping a friend, but he also knew this was merely a distraction. Time was running out. By now, his father would have realized he left town and would be disowning him.

FEAR AND LOATHING
in Punta Cana

"That swine! I knew it! Living on three hundred thousand euros for five years? I knew that was impossible. I fell for his charms. How did he do it? Paper in the safe jamb? A shim in the door?" Bria writhed with anger. How could she have been so stupid? Bria didn't know where to start but she knew the first step would be to report the crime. She marched up the crooked little walkway to the receptionist's desk. "I need to talk to security," she barked.

Security responded, but not with any answers she was expecting.

"No, ma'am, we don't have cameras there."

"No, ma'am, we don't guarantee your belongings. Did you not see the sign in your room, you must lock your valuables in the safe, ma'am."

"No, ma'am, we are not liable if the safe is broken."

"No, ma'am, we don't have a fingerprint kit."

The angrier Bria got, the more demanding she became. Every ounce of money or access to money was gone and all these clowns could do was apologize and say,

"No, ma'am."

They agreed to call the police but assured her that they would give her similar answers. Her belongings were gone. They would most likely just file a report.

And then she got the answer that would change her anger to fear— "No, ma'am, we don't keep a copy of your license or passport."

"Well why would you ask for it? Surely you wrote the number down?"

"No, Ma'am. I am very sorry."

Bria's head spun as she heard the words. What would she do next? She stood, unable to move or speak, for what seemed like an eternity.

"Ma'am? Ma'am? Are you all right?" She heard the words peripherally. Fear was ricocheting through her brain. What would she do next? How would she get home? How would she survive on the island with no money?

"Ma'am? Ms. Brigante?"

Bria could hear the guard speaking but couldn't answer. Finally, she quietly mouthed the words, "Can you give me a ride to the consulate?" Was that even where she should go? Bria's mind continued to race.

"I'm sorry, ma'am. Did you say something?"

"The consulate," Bria repeated, "I need a ride to the consulate."

"Of course, ma'am" replied the employee.

"I need to go back to my room and make some calls. Can I meet you up here in one hour?" She was polite again. Hopelessness overcame her.

The walk back to the cottage was shorter than she remembered. She wouldn't recall much more than the counting of bills from her swimsuit top. One, two, three, eight, eighteen, thirty-eight dollars. She'd count it again, hoping the twenties were stuck together. Twenty. Thirty. Thirty-five. Thirty-six, seven, eight. What would she do with thirty-eight dollars? That wouldn't even cover the cash she would need for the trip home. She would call Julia the minute she got inside. Something was going on with Julia, but she would help her out of this mess. She could always count on Julia.

She looked at the hotel phone and the instructions plastered to the face of the old, acrylic, push-button relic. She could barely make out the instructions. "Push nine and then zero…" she read out loud. Julia picked up on the first ring, "Hello?"

"Julia, I'm so glad you picked up! I need your..."

The phone clicked. Had Julia hung up on her? She called back immediately. The phone rang once and was sent to voicemail. "I think we have a bad connection, Jules, it's Bri. I've been robbed and they stole my money, my ID, everything... I just don't know what to do. You're the level-headed one in our relationship. Jules, call me. I need you..." Bria read the number of the hotel into the receiver and asked her to have her paged. She also reminded her of her email address.

Bria picked up the receiver a second time and dialed Brad at the office. She held her breath as she got Virginia, his admin, on the line. "Virginia, can I talk to Brad? It's an emergency."

There was silence for a moment, and then, "Brianna?"

"Yes, Virginia, it's Bria. Can I talk to Brad?"

"I'm sorry, Bria, he's told me not to send your calls through." Bria tried to remain calm. She tried to remember about flies and vinegar, but she wanted to erupt.

"Virginia, I'm sorry for the email, but this is an emergency." Virginia paused, as if wondering what to do.

"Hold on, dear. Let me get him." While she waited, Bria was surprised by Virginia's eagerness to help. Maybe she felt guilty for what she had done?

"Brianna?"

"Yes, Virginia, I'm still here."

"I'm so sorry, dear, Brad won't take your call."

"Did you tell him it was an emergency?"

"I did. I'm sorry. I could tell by your voice that it's dire. I tried to tell him, but he just said no. I'm so sorry, Brianna."

Bria wanted to scream. This was her fault. She couldn't understand Virginia's tone. Why was she being so kind? Bria's temper got the best of her, "Virginia, this wouldn't be happening if you didn't share that email! I need Brad and I need him NOW!"

Virginia responded coolly, "I didn't, and that's no way to talk to someone who's trying to help you." At that, Bria heard her hang up and the dial tone returned in her ear.

Bria sat on the polyester coverlet staring at the strewn clothes escaping the dresser drawers. She'd call Julia again tomorrow, she thought. She'd have a better idea of how she could help after going to the consulate. Maybe she could email her now? Could she remember her email address? She would email Brad. It was at that moment that Bria was reminded that she had no one else. She sat alone on the bed, tears streaming down her cheeks.

"Papà," she whispered.

Brianna Brigante was completely alone.

WOMAN HUNT

"Did you find her?"

"I will. Does the boss know I lost her?"

"No, not yet. You better hurry up, Vegas. Did she make you at the airport?"

"No. I blend right in with the tourists around here." Vinny looked at his new look—he couldn't wait to get back into something more respectable. He was happy to have so much hair on his arms and legs or he'd really stand out with his pale skin. His parents were both Italian, but his mother was fair-skinned from northern Italy. Growing up they called him Whitey, but you never want to be named after a made man, especially that one. Vinny paid a couple hood rats to start calling him "Vinny Vegas" and it eventually stuck.

"How'd you get through security with your piece, Vegas?"

"I had to drop it."

"I'll have my guy down there get you a new one, leave your phone on and I'll tell you where ta meet 'im."

"Got it."

"You got a piece already?"

"No, asshole. I got your message, I'll leave my phone on." Vinny's voice raised in irritation. "What da fuck?" he continued mumbling, his pinky ring tapping angrily against the phone as he spoke.

He hung up the phone, "Where is this fucking kid?"

THE BARTENDER

This could be fun, Devon thought, as he strolled past the pool looking at the rows of beautiful women. At least it was a distraction, until he figured out what to do next with his life. Just saying those words in his head seemed overwhelming. If he were going to defy his father, whatever he decided needed to be big.

The pool was at capacity. He thought about Max's concerns. Could someone be stealing? Devon walked down the beautiful promenade toward the beach. He was assigned to the beach bar. As he approached the bar, he noticed a strong white wood frame with a mixture of teak, novelty thatching on the roof, and the same white sheer curtains that flowed in the lobby. It was straight out of *Afar* magazine with luxury oozing from the exotic wood bar. Oddly, unlike the crowded pool bar, this bar had only one customer. The customer seemed focused on watching passersby more than partaking in idle chitchat with the lone barkeep. This worked well as the bored employee took his time explaining the set up to Devon.

"Thanks for the tour," said Devon.

"No problem. Hope you're not getting paid by the drink out here, mate." His new friend said as he stepped out of the bar.

As the barkeep stepped away, he stopped abruptly. He stepped in closer to Devon,

"Hey, I forgot to mention this. You need to keep the locals out of the bar, they have to stay beyond the railing."

"We don't serve locals?" Devon pondered out loud.

"If they have money, yes. If they want money, no. If you have any trouble, call security. They're used to dealing with them." Devon looked out toward the beach. There were dozens of pristine white cabanas organized between palm trees. They were perfectly designed to take in the Caribbean breeze and views. Some had sofas and chairs with indulgent white cushions and blue and white striped accent pillows. Some had luxurious blue mattresses with long, rolled cushions that would perfectly prop the most discriminating head. Two cabanas had anchored crystal chandeliers over teak dining sets. A romantic setting for dinner. But still, every cabana was empty— but one. In the occupied cabana, an older couple sat alone, surrounded by several beach vendors. Again, Bria wasn't sure for whom she felt more sorry— the vendors or the couple trying to enjoy a romantic evening. A lone waiter stood poised on the edge of the beach leaning against a massive palm, awaiting a guest to serve. Devon couldn't understand why no one took advantage of this luxury.

Alone behind the bar, Devon decided to start a conversation with his lone patron.

"It's pretty sweet out here, isn't it? Can I get you a refill?"

His patron barely moved his gaze from the beach. Without looking, he slid his empty glass toward Devon, tapping lightly on the glass with his clunky pinky ring. Devon remembered the man being at Newark with his gold chains and ring.

"What are you drinking, sir?" Devon was trying to remember what bartenders had asked him as recently as yesterday. He continued looking at the ring and how his round fingers puffed out around it.

"Give me another one of those rum things, with the fruit." Devon tried to hide his stare. Could that be the same man from the airport? It was a couple days ago. He was watching that gold digger intently. But what was his story? Devon couldn't help but wonder.

A young couple came to the bar next.

"It's beautiful," the girl said as she gazed into her lover's eyes. Devon wasn't a big fan of PDA but was thankful for the time to go unnoticed as he figured out how to make her drink—

a bushwacker.

Devon had a total of ten customers, never more than two at one time. He started cleaning up the barely used bar as his shift came to an end.

"Brothah!" his new valet friend was walking by with a few other employees. Devon waved. The group kept walking and Devon knew he needed to act fast.

"You guys headed to a party I wasn't invited to?" he yelled, reminded of his frat house days.

"Yes. You come, too, brotha. We'll just be doing a little celebrating down the way. Come when you're done."

"I'll be there." Devon shouted back with a smile.

He knew this group wasn't sophisticated enough to be stealing millions of dollars, but he knew getting close to them might shed some light on strange behavior or "clean ups" — as one of his Wharton professors would call them. A clean up was when the suspect knew he was going to be put under a microscope, so he starts ordering the team to complete unusual tasks to cover his tracks before the investigation. He— or they— would ask employees to create duplicate files, physically move office supplies or boxes, or delete files with strange names. They could also start implanting false memories. For example, they might ask several employees if they remember a certain client and then tell a similar story to each one. This way, when someone asked the team if they remembered a particular guest, the team would honestly say things like, "Wow, that name seems familiar," or, "Oh yes! I remember him." In many cases, there was never such a person. Being new, Devon was perfectly positioned to ask his coworkers how they had spent their day and maybe even solicit strange orders from bosses.

Still, Devon couldn't help but get the man with the pinky ring out of his head. He was shady, for sure. He doubted he would have anything to do with the problems at Blooming Sands, but Devon would watch him just the same.

EMBASSY BOUND

"Santo Domingo is two and a half hours from Punta Cana, señorita," explained the Caribe security guard assigned to the problem. "I'm bringing you to Expreso Bavaro where you can get the bus. It's four hundred pesos."

"What?" Bria shouted. "You're not bringing me there? This is your fault! This theft happened on your property. No, you will drive me to Santo Domingo." The young man stood speechless, one hand on her door, his mouth agape.

"No, no, señorita. I was told to bring you to Expreso Bavaro," he pleaded. Bria was too irritated to accept no for an answer. She leaned over him sternly, her father's spirit running through her veins.

"You do not want to find out what happens when you don't do what I ask."

Silence.

The strapping young security guard could not believe his eyes. He struggled to find any words.

"I will have to check—" finally sputtered from his lips.

"No. You don't." Bria stood firm.

She turned to the valet, and just as firmly ordered him to follow her order. "You. Go tell your manager that..." Bria paused to look at the young man's name badge, "Orlando will be driving Miss Brigante to Santo Domingo and he shouldn't expect him back for several hours." The valet somehow knew not to question the order and nodded his head. Bria turned to the security guard, "Are you clear? Let's go." Her command of the situation left both employees stunned. There was a sureness in her tone that left both men speechless. It wasn't her beauty, but something else.

The first twenty minutes Bria and her escort drove in silence. The dust from the road filled the old van. The bench seats that were organized in rows behind the driver took every bump with a bounce and Bria could feel the old springs penetrating her sundress. She moved back a seat in hopes the next seat would be gentler. The next bump sent her flying out of her seat. It would be a long two hours. She looked at the old map that filled the seat next to the driver. She walked up to the front of the van, leaned over the driver's shoulder and demanded he pull over. She got out of the back of the van and moved to the front seat.

The road to Santo Domingo turned smooth and more like a highway than she had expected. Punta Cana was rural with cinder block one-room homes and caged dogs in bodegas. The road they were now on, was well-traveled with a far more modern landscape of which she hadn't expected. As they neared the city, the young man's face lit up. Had he never been here before? Bria wondered. A crop of high rises appeared in the horizon and she could feel from his energy that he was excited to be there.

As they maneuvered the traffic, cars and pedestrians began filling the streets. Following the young man's GPS, they circled a rotary just to do it once more when he missed his turn. As they turned to what Bria identified as old Santo Domingo, Bria found yet another surprise. A whole other world existed on the far side of the island. Colorful buildings in soft pastels lined brick and cobblestone streets. A daffodil and white wood building with a wrought iron balcony stood elegantly, first in a row of buildings on the quaint street. It seemed to complement the sienna painted stucco of its attached neighbor. A restaurant was filled with diners and filled the crowded sidewalk. Bria imagined finding her money and having lunch on their front patio. The next building, a muted pink, was elegant with tall gothic windows, but sat slightly crooked next to the other two. Building after building lined the street with far softer Caribbean hues than she noticed in Punta Cana. At the end of the street, where the tourist attraction ended and the neighborhood began, several students kicked a ball. Their uniforms, knee length khaki skirts with Caribbean blue button-downs matching their socks, added to the feel of the quaint old town. Bria wished she could walk the streets and explore the shops but knew she had more pressing business. Bria had five days left to figure out how to get home before she'd miss her flight.

The U.S. Embassy sat far from the quaint town on a massive expanse of lush, green land. It was intimidating. It was far from what Bria had expected. As the hotel van puttered onto the grounds, a team of security guards greeted the pair. After a barrage of metal detectors, wands and questions, Bria finally made her way to the information line inside. The line was long, and dozens upon dozens sat waiting their turn with small numbered slips. Bria couldn't imagine why they all waited. A small boy held the hem of his mother's skirt as she sat rocking his baby sister on the hard bench. His nose was highlighted by the dried mucous that dried white around each nostril against his dark skin. Surely, they weren't all missing passports? She wondered how many were American. There were few fair-skinned people waiting, but that meant nothing. Asylum? The Dominican didn't seem very threatening. She tried to imagine why scores of people sat filling every bench and on the hard floor with their backs resting on the cold marble wall. What they were waiting for? Bria couldn't be sure, but the idea that they were waiting was concerning enough. At the head of the line, a Dominican woman in an official blue button-down with a U.S. Embassy patch took Bria's name and asked why she was there. Bria explained what happened and the woman handed her a number and a piece of paper. On the top of the paper was the U.S. seal and the words "LOST OR STOLEN PASSPORT."

It read:

"In the event that your passport is lost or stolen, first report the theft to the local police in order to get a police report. Along with the police report, you will need proof of citizenship and a photo ID, such as a driver's license, school ID (for minors) or a Dominican ID-cédula (for dual nationals)."

Bria's heart sank. She knew there had to be provisions for such a thing as having no ID, but it was not anywhere on this list. There was then another list of directions below that listed required documentation:

Application form DSP-11 completed ONLINE and printed. Hand-written filled application forms are NOT accepted. Applications are NOT to be signed until you are requested to do so by a Consular Officer.

Form DS-64 (Report of a lost or stolen passport) completed ONLINE and printed. Hand-written filled application forms are NOT accepted.

Attach two 2×2 inch photos. For your convenience, photos can be obtained inside the Consular waiting area.

Any identification available to prove your citizenship accompanied by a photocopy of each one, for example: previous passport and a copy, naturalization certificate and copy, certificate of citizenship and a copy. If available, bring a copy of the lost or stolen passport. In Santo Domingo, copies can be obtained inside the Consular waiting area. At the Consular Agencies, please bring copies to the interview with you.

As if the list of requirements Bria would be unable to fill was overwhelming, the final bullet made her catch her breath:

Fee.

So far, she had a police report. That was it. She also had a hotel key, thirty-eight dollars, and a somewhat willing hostage who might vouch for her identity.

The last thing on the list worried her: a fee. She turned to the woman, "How much is the fee?"

The busy employee stated, "One hundred forty-five dollars if you don't need notaries, ma'am."

"And if I do?" asked Bria.

"Oh, maybe it would be ninety? Maybe one hundred thirty-five? Everyone is different senora."

"What if I don't have any identification at all? It was all stolen." Bria held her breath while awaiting the answer.

"Well, ma'am. You will need to make an appointment in our Punta Cana location for an interview. They will help you."

"Punta Cana?? I just came from Punta Cana." Bria was enraged. Her hotel not only didn't keep her belongings safe, but now they wasted over five hours of her time driving to an Embassy when there is one just miles from her hotel? She looked at her security guard, he was oblivious to the problem.

"How do I get an appointment?" Bria asked. The woman handed her another piece of paper. It read:

If you would like to make an appointment at one of the Consular Agencies, please email Punta Cana Consular Agency or Puerto Plata Consular Agency. If you experience technical difficulties or do not have access to internet, you may make your appointment by calling (809) 552-8990 for Punta Cana or calling telephone numbers (809) 586-8017, (809) 586-4204, (809) 586-8023 for Puerto Plata. To make an appointment for services in Santo Domingo, please click on the following link to go directly to our online appointment system.

Bria took a deep breath. "How long does that take?"

"Oh, one month, maybe two? It's best to have a friend send you your ID from the states and fill out the form." The woman was trying to be kind, but her frustration grew as the line behind Bria grew longer with each question.

"Well, what if my money was stolen as well?" Bria asked with a thread of hopefulness left.

"Well, ma'am, maybe you should ask your friend to send you some of that as well." She didn't mean to sound rude, but Bria's eyes glassed over.

"You'll be all right miss, I can tell. Don't you worry. You just go back to your hotel and call your family. You'll be all right." The woman tried to console her but Bria's eyes teared more.

She mouthed "Thank you" and gave the woman a soft smile. She walked toward her security guard and motioned for them to leave. She wanted to berate the young man. She wanted to kick and scream and demand the hotel fix this. Bria wasn't sure if it was the situation or the fact that she had no one to call that made her more emotional. She hopped into the back of the old van and laid down across the very back seat and wept.

Bria got back to her room and checked for messages. None. She wondered how people lived without cell phones. She knew she needed to check her email. Hopefully Julia had sent her an email and already had a plan. She had also sent out a few resumes before she left, it would be good to see if anyone had responded. Her only access had been her phone, which was now gone and sorely missed. Bria laid on the bed, staring at the ceiling of her hotel room. She was tired; really tired. She tried to muster the energy to go back to the lobby and ask for the business center, but exhaustion filled her, and her body refused to move. She had not eaten anything all day and her hunger and her emotions were paralyzing her. She decided to go to the hotel restaurant and have something better than the tiresome buffet she had been living on because of its proximity to the bar. Bria mustered up the strength to stand up and didn't as much as brush her hair before walking down the crooked cobblestone.

She worked through the timeline in her head. If Julia could get her what she needed by Wednesday, she could book the appointment at the consulate for Thursday. She may have enough time before her flight left on Friday. It was late. Bria looked at the clock next to the bed. They had barely made it to the Embassy by four-thirty and it was now closing in on nine o'clock. Nothing would happen tonight.

She dialed Julia's number from her hotel room one more time before leaving for dinner. Again, two rings and the phone was sent to voicemail. Hopefully Julia was OK? This was completely out of character, not to mention Julia was Bria's last hope. Bria counted the days she had left.

VINNY

"I don't know where she is, boss, but I'll find her."
"You'd better, Vegas."
"I will, boss."
"Call me the minute you do."

Vinny went for another walk on the beach. He was positive she said Punta Cana. Twenty miles of beachfront and all he had found was a sunburn and sore legs. "Hopefully she didn't make a run for it," he thought. Vinny looked at the list of hotels in Punta Cana with the word Caribe in them. There were sixteen. Not insurmountable, but not an easy task either. He listed them in order of star reviews with the best on top. "This is not a simple girl," Vinny would continuously remind himself. His frustration was getting the best of him as he stroked the twenty-two caliber gun hidden in his shorts.

"A twenty-two?" He had asked his contact when they met.

"What the hell am I supposed to do with a twenty-two, tattoo her? The only thing this is good for is keeping those fucking beach vendors away from me."

The man shrugged, "That's all I have, man. Maybe I come back later wit somethin' bigger?"

Vinny was still waiting for his island connection to call. One thing he was learning about this island? Time moves slowly for everyone but Vinny.

"Boss, I'll find her." Vinny could not stop thinking about his last words to his boss. He'd better find her. This was not the sort of business where you get away with letting down your boss.

FOUR DAYS LEFT

Bria woke with a start. Was it all a bad dream? She looked at the phone for the eightieth time in six hours. The light had still not lit up. No messages. She'd grab a cup of coffee and then head to the lobby and find the business center. There had to be a message from Julia there.

For the first time, Bria grabbed whatever clothes found their way to her hand. She didn't care what she looked like. She had four days left and thirty-eight dollars.

Bria found herself infuriated by the crooked paths this morning. She was tired of weaving around obstacles; she wanted a straight line somewhere. Her father never worked around things. When he wanted something, he went directly after it. As she followed the arrow she found at the crossroads of crooked paths, it directed her to the lobby. She promised to write this new lesson in her leather journal. "Don't waste time on crooked paths," she whispered out loud.

Upon entering the lobby, Bria noticed a fresh set of plastic cups awaiting the next round of tourists. They were freshly made and lacked the watery cap that rested on the ones that greeted her when she arrived. It made her long for a cocktail. Something to wash the pain of the week away. Should she go to the bar? No, she convinced herself. No more crooked lines. Alcohol had only helped her deviate from her path. Her new resolve to stay straight would need to keep her focused. There would be a time for a drink, and that time was not now.

When Bria entered the small room to the right of the check-in desk, an antiquated computer sitting alone on a simple wood table greeted her. In the corner of the room sat a small table with an old printer and several stacked reams of printer paper beneath it. A phone similar to the one in her garden suite was the only other thing in the room. Bria stepped out of the room, prepared to at least fix one thing today. Noticing a chair that had been tucked behind the check-in counter, she marched behind the counter and rolled the chair into the small room with the computer.

As Bria waited for the computer to turn on, she picked up the phone and tried to call Julia again. The phone clicked over to an operator who informed her that her credit card on file had been declined and she would have to call collect. Furious, Bria demanded the operator connect her.

Bria heard Julia pick up the phone. As if in an old movie, Julia couldn't hear Bria as the operator chimed in over Bria's voice asking, "Will you accept a collect call from Bria?"

"No, no I won't."

"Julia, Julia! What's going on! Talk to me! What the hell is going on?" Bria desperately tried to be heard but it was no use. The call was disconnected with a simple,

"I'm sorry, ma'am," from the operator.

Bria couldn't believe what she had just heard. Tears filled her eyes. Bria sat motionless and stunned. In the background, the computer in front of her hummed and buzzed acknowledging its readiness. Bria couldn't stop staring at the phone. "What had just happened?" Bria's mind raced with the question. She sat motionless hearing the words repeat in her head, "No, no I won't." Sure, every friend had riffs, but very rarely did Bria and Julia even disagree.

The computer screen in front of Bria went dark again, snapping Bria out of her trance while her hand reflexively tapped the keyboard.

"Why?" Bria knew that was the first thing she would type.

Bria opened her mail to find her unmanaged inbox filled with emails from solicitors. As she scrolled past the spam, she found her first email from Vicci. In the subject line, the word

"Bitch" sat alone. The next email was from an unknown gmail account with the subject line, "Thank you." Bria opened it to find a scathing letter from a woman she didn't know calling her a whore. Bria would read enough to know that Bria had slept with her husband. She quickly deleted it, shrugging off the assertion that it was in any way her fault. "Men are pigs," she'd remind herself. DELETE. Bria kept scrolling until she found an email from the Hoyer Agency. The subject line read, "Your application for employment." Finally, some good news. Bria opened it immediately.

Shocked, she read, "Based on your magnanimous and divisive public profile, we feel that you are not a good fit for our agency at this time. Best of luck." DELETE.

She didn't know why she deleted the email so fast, but she couldn't handle rejection. With that said, she wouldn't forget the words they chose, "Magnanimous and divisive public profile."

Bria tried to shake off the turndown. Perhaps it was someone who has a connection at Vicci? Shock followed when a similar response showed up further down in her inbox.

"We have a strict policy about public communication and reputation. At this time, we'll have to pass." DELETE.

Bria found three more further down in her inbox. DELETE. DELETE. DELETE.

A machine gun of questions fire within her. *Could this all be because of my inter-office email? How could everyone have known? What about my results? My campaigns are amazing! How could one saucy email to my boss negate the millions of dollars I've brought to the agency?*

This was what she had left: her career. This was the only thing she had left.

Bria tries to harness the prize-fighter within her. "I'll fix this later." She turns her focus to Julia and Brad. Surely one of them would come through. Brad had professed his love to Bria. Julia was the only one who meant anything to Bria anymore. Someone would help.

She notices an email from Julia dated yesterday morning, right after her first call was denied. The subject line was strange. It just said, "EMAIL." Inside, the email held more mystery.

Brianna,
Based on your recent call, I can see you haven't been checking your emails. The answer is no. No help, no conversation, no. I will never talk to you again.
Julia

Bria is shocked. What is she talking about?

She quickly scrolls through her inbox and finds an email from BVicci@gmail.com. Brad! In the subject line he's written, "NOT CONFIDENTIAL."

Bria is relieved to see he's contacted her. She ignored the strange subject line and opened the email. The first page is filled with the email addresses of everyone else copied on the email. There were close to two hundred people on the list.

"What is this?" Bria asked quietly.

She scrolls down and sees a series of thirty or forty small boxes on the screen trying to download. The first box is named "The Letter." Each of the remaining boxes were labeled with men's names. The first four were labeled "Brad Vicci 1," "Brad Vicci 2," "Brad Vicci 3," and "Brad Vicci 4." Below it, she found similar labels but with different names.

The first box finally downloaded. Bria sees a copy of the email to Brad that was shared throughout the company. While the next picture downloads, she scrolled back up to the "cc:" box. She found the name of every advertising agency she knows, and some she didn't, listed in the body of email addresses. She scrolled back down to the downloading icons.

A picture of Brad's naked body standing in Bria's bedroom window opens. "Brad Vicci 1."

Bria waits for the second, it reveals Bria wrapping her arms around Brad and holding his erect cock. Three reveals her going down on him. Bria catches her breath. She scrolls down to the list of names. Three quarters of the way down, she sees "Doug McVerry 1." Tears start pouring from her eyes. Her memory started rushing back. She had pushed it out of her mind. The picture opened, helping fill in the gaps in Bris's memory.

It was a picture of Bria and Doug in Bria's apartment. Bria had forgotten about that drunk night after Julia and Doug were separated. Bria was so drunk she could barely walk. Doug had found her outside trying to hail a cab when he "came to her rescue"—in more ways than one. Bria's memory of the evening was patchy. Although she didn't remember having sex with Doug, her body had told her she betrayed her best friend in the morning.

In the picture, Doug was carrying Bria into the bedroom and kissing her. She was clothed, and you couldn't see her face well. The second picture opened to Doug standing at the end of her bed, naked and erect, and Bria looking back laughing. The third showed them on the bed, Bria's dress hiked up to her waist and her breasts thrust through her low-cut dress. Her full breasts stood tall and erect as the cut of the dress seemed to display them perfectly and present them to Doug's eager mouth. Doug's hand disappeared between her legs. The next picture showed his penetration. Bria scrolled back to the top of the page. JMcVerry12@aol.com. Julia.

It was clear that someone had hired a private investigator to follow Bria. But who? These were sent from Brad's email. It couldn't have been Brad, the pictures only hurt him and his business. Brad's wife?

Bria didn't wait for the rest to open. She couldn't believe what she had just seen. She raced back to Julia's email and hit reply. There was nothing more important than this moment. She started her email explaining the situation, her drunkenness, that they were separated, how he took advantage of her… and then she stopped. She held the backspace button down while she cried and then wrote:

Jules,

Shakespeare says it is better to have loved and lost than to never have loved. He must never have experienced the love I have for you. I am treacherously sorry, my dear friend. I'll pray to my father and to our Father to help us find our way back, but in the event we don't, and I don't deserve that we should, know I love you more than my own. You have been the greatest gift I have ever known. I love you and I'm sorry, sorry far beyond any words I could write.
Brianna Brigante

She hit send. Bria didn't want to read any more. She didn't want to look at any more pictures. Those were crooked paths, she thought. "Crooked paths led me here." It was still early in the day, but she could think of nothing but Julia. It wasn't loneliness setting upon her now. Loneliness was having to spend time alone. Loneliness was not taking the time to make friends. This emotion, this was the loss of the last person she has ever loved. Julia Strichorn McVerry was her soul.

Bria was empty. She didn't know where to go or what to do. There was no passport trauma, she didn't care about money, she didn't even care about what she would do for a living. This mistake was greater than any other.

She happened on the crooked path until it opened up to the pool. She looked down at what she wore: cut-off distressed shorts, a tight T-shirt, and a big hat in which she had lobbed her long hair in her haste. She wanted desperately to walk through the pool and sit at the dirty bar and down mamajuanas until she couldn't see. The bartender looked up at her but didn't make his usual call to her. Bria paused, but then walked straight past the bar to the beach. She sat directly on the sand, near the water's edge.

Wave after wave broke on the beach in front of Bria. Twice, she had to move back as the tide came in. She watched two white playeritos play in the surf as she wallowed. As the waves broke, the small birds would run along the foam from the surf, furiously capturing any little treasure they could from the sand. They'd be so busy fighting for their livelihood, but in the midst of their work, would take a minute to touch beaks. It was as if they were thoughtfully reminding each other that they were still there, together.

Hours passed as Bria didn't move. Vendor after vendor approached her as she sat watching, alone. Bria ignored them. They'd swarm around her trying to sell their wares, yet Bria's gaze never left the sea. Her mind never left Julia. She didn't bother with her standard, "No tengo dinero," because right now, she had less than that.

As Bria's legs started to burn from the sun, she rose from the sand to find her way back to the hotel. She was suddenly stopped by who was in front of her.

That man. He had just passed her, but she knew him. He was short and stocky and carried driving loafers in his hand. How did she know him? Maybe he didn't, she reasoned. He would have stopped and said something. Was it the same man she saw the other night from her window? She was sure her mind was playing tricks on her and headed back to the hotel.

As Bria reached the shade, she pulled off her hat and let her hair flow free.

"Mamajuana? One little sip, Señorita Bria?" the bartender called. Bria smiled and walked straight to the crooked path. She knew she needed to get Julia off her mind. Her priority needed to be getting home. To do that, she would need money and ID. It was becoming increasingly clear that this was not something that Julia, or any one else, was going to help her attain. This meant, in four days, Bria would be homeless, broke, and trapped in Punta Cana.

She would need to find that thieving gigolo. Bria was sure he wasn't going to stroll by and visit after what he had done, so finding him might be a little more difficult. She would also need some money. Could she talk some rich vacationer into buying her more than a drink?

Bria opened the door to her cottage and looked around. What would she do?

UNDERCOVER

"Max, it's Devon. Can you hear me? I'm walking on the beach, I didn't want anyone to overhear anything at the hotel."

"Yeah, Buddy, what'd you find?" Max was eager for an update.

"I've found a few small things, but— hey, no, no, I don't want anything— sorry buddy, a sand flea— I've found a—"

"What? A sand flea?" Max asked, "Sun getting to you, Devon?"

"Yea, you know, these damn beach vendors. There're all over, trying to sell you cheap souvenirs and bad paintings. When you walk the beach here you can't escape them," Devon informed his friend. "Anyway, there's a few small things, some petty theft of food and beer, but nothing that adds up to what we're talking about. There's a woman in HR I think will go on a date with me. I'm going to see if I can get anywhere with her."

"Well don't fall in love, I don't need two of you screwing me!" Max chuckled. "Thanks man."

"No problem. We'll figure— damn— no, go away! We'll figure this out quickly."

"Sand flea?"

"Yeah, how'd you know?" Devon chuckled.

"Next time, wear some repellent, brah!" At that, both men laughed and agreed to reconnect in a couple days.

THE JOURNAL

Bria opened her journal. In it, she read the previous notes she had made and added her newest revelation to the following page. She looked straight ahead in the mirror that showcased a disheveled woman, a polyester coverlet with island flowers, and a cheap bamboo backdrop. Brianna didn't know this woman. She struggled to see anyone she knew looking back at her. Everything she knew was gone. Bria looked at this woman who had been holding onto the past. She had been holding on to her family that once was. She was holding on to a friendship that once was. She was holding on to the anger that was caused by losing one and pushing the second away.

Bria looked down at the empty journal. "Papà, I wish you had filled these empty pages with me before you left me." She fanned the pages as she thought of all the lessons she would need to learn in order to fill them.

Did she see something?

She fanned the pages again. Her father had written more. She fanned the pages slower. She stopped when she saw writing.

A carne di lupo, zanne di cane.

" A carne di lupo, zanne di cane." Bria read out loud. You must meet roughness with roughness. Was that the translation? At that, a loud caw came from her patio. She looked out to the railing and a small hawk sat on the back of the patio chair looking in. Its light brown eyes penetrated Bria's. Its feathers were fine, and its light grey coloring was much different than the brown hawks she remembered from New Jersey. This bird had a bright yellow bridge across its hooked beak. Papà would always say hawks are messengers of the angels. They would help you see more clearly. This hawk was like no other she had ever seen. Since her father's death, when she was at Wharton and even in the city, Bria begged for a hawk to visit her. Here she was, at her most low, and Papà sent a harbinger.

"Help me see, Papà." Bria prayed to the bird.

The bird sat, staring at Bria. Neither moved. Bria hoped to have some divine inspiration leap from the beak of the hawk. What had she expected? His eyes were menacing but welcoming. She wanted to walk toward him. Would it lead her somewhere? Bria rose from the bed and the creek from the springy mattress scared her messenger. He jumped to a nearby bush.

"What are you telling me, little friend?"

His eyes continued to glare. Bria opened the patio door and he remained in position. She hit the metal chair with her foot as she focused on the creature. The noise forced an almost vertical exit to the top of the tress. It was gone. He was gone. Bria looked back at the leather-bound journal, and then up to the trees. Her heart felt lighter, somehow. She could do this.

A carne di lupo, zanne di cane.

Bria flipped through further pages of the book where she found three more pages with her father's handwriting.

The next said,

A chi vuole, non mancano modi. Where there is a will, there is a way.

The next made Bria laugh out loud, *Al buon vino non bisogna frasca.* This translated to "Good wine needs no bush." Every time Bria talked about becoming a world-famous advertising executive, her father would merely respond,

"Al buon vino non bisogna frasca."

It was only when she graduated that she learned what it

really meant: A good product does not need advertising. Her father didn't want her to go into advertising; he wanted her to go into the family business.

The last quote he left her was the strangest.

Aiutati che Dio ti aiuta

"'Help yourself, and God will help you.' Oh Papà, you're full of surprises." She and her father regularly sparred about God. They were Roman Catholic, but Papà would never go to church with the family. When Bria would challenge him, Papà would only say,

"You'll understand one day, my Bella. But you, Bella, you be good for God and He will be good to you. You listen to your mama and Father Franconi, okay?"

Bria looked again at the woman in the mirror. 'A carne di lupo, zanne di cane,' she said. The woman suddenly looked different.

Bria showered and put on her smartest outfit. Who knew she'd be going on a job interview in the Dominican Republic? Even the hotel manager didn't know what to expect. Bria put together her least provocative outfit, which was a challenge with her long legs and propensity to highlight them. She marched up the crooked path to the front desk.

"Puedo hablar con el gerente?" Bria's Spanish was rusty, but she commanded respect despite it.

"Un momento, por favor, señorita," the front clerk responded.

A few moments later, an unremarkable man with a mustache emerged from the back office. "Buenos dias. Como puedo ayudarte?" he said meekly. His Spanish was not as good as Bria's.

"Señor, I would like to discuss some solutions with you. I'm sure you're aware of my situation? My name is Brianna Brigante."

"Ahh, yes, Miss Brigante. I've heard of your troubles."

Bria continued to pitch the manager on hiring her, to support marketing the hotel in exchange for continuing her stay and a small salary. She pledged a remarkable ad campaign for the resort that would save him thousands upon thousands of dollars and help increase his sales.

She waited for his response proudly.

"Well, all of this sounds lovely, Miss Brigante. I'd really like to help you considering the situation but, as it turns out, we haven't advertised in over five years and we haven't had a vacant room in six."

Bria wasn't going to be stopped. "Well, I believe a smart campaign could improve the quality of guest and increase your top line revenue."

"I'm sorry, Miss Brigante. We've had this conversation with some of Madison Avenue's finest associates. If we elevate the quality of our guest, we must then elevate the quality of our rooms, our pool, our towels, our staff, and even our food. Today, we offer the best deal in the Caribbean and give young people a lot of food and alcohol for their dollar. We think our current strategy is making wonderful vacations accessible to those who might otherwise not be able to afford them." Bria thought about her maxed out credit card as he said this.

Bria started to do what she does best and counter his argument. The manager simply raised his finger to silence her, "I am sincerely sorry, Señorita Brigante, but your room is also fully booked. I won't be able to allow you to stay on, but I hope you enjoy the few days you have left at Caribe Resort."

And that was it.

The manager smiled cordially, slightly bowed, and walked back into his office, leaving Bria standing dumbfounded in the lobby. Bria looked over to the welcome table, at the three plastic cups that remained standing with their melted ice discoloring the tropical punch. This was not the place she wanted to be.

"Act the part you want, Bria," she advised herself. Bria turned and walked back toward her room.

"FUCK!" she yelled as she moved out of eyesight.

Bria noticed the maid in the bungalow next to hers. She had an idea. Bria walked in her neighbor's room, calling for the housekeeper. Seeing her in the bathroom, she walked right in, past the bathroom and into the bedroom area.

"Señora, did you see anyone in my bungalow when my things were taken?" The housekeeper looked horrified. Bria explained, "No, no, I am not blaming you. I just need to find the man, the person, so I can get my passport back and get home."

"No señorita, I see nothing. I'm so sorry." She was nervous.

"Well, I think I know who did it." The housekeeper froze. Bria was surprised by her response but kept talking. "I just want to know which way he went when he left or if you've seen him? He's about this tall, nice looking, Italian, long hair like Fabio, but brown. You know Fabio?"

"Yes," the housekeeper blushed. "I know Fabio. He no stay at Resort Caribe!" She laughed, finally relaxing. Bria smiled.

"If you see him, will you tell me right away?"

"I will, I will, señorita."

"It's Bria. Thank you... Vivian?" Bria smiled that warm, genuine smile and went to leave. While leaving, she knocked over the suitcase on the stand. "Oh no! I'm so sorry."

The maid rushed to pick it up. "Oh no, oh no," she muttered.

While she was distracted, Bria unlocked the adjoining door. "I'm sorry, if they say something, I will let them know it was my fault, Vivian. I'm so sorry. Thank you, Vivian."

Bria walked next door to see her room had already been cleaned. She listened carefully as she heard Vivian muttering under her breath and then make a phone call. She could hear her talking but couldn't make out any of her words. Finally, she heard the door close behind her.

Bria had seen the couple next door several times. She decided to take a quick walk to the pool to see if she could spot them. Sure enough, they were just being pulled in for what looked like their first mamajuana of the afternoon. "Perfect!" Bria walked briskly back to her room where she got right to work. She put the chain on her front door as she entered. She moved quickly to the adjoining door, thrilled to find it still unlocked. She moved quickly through the couple's room to attach the chain on their door as well. She then opened the back porch just a crack, making it look as if this was how someone had entered. Then she quickly got to work.

First things first, she needed to call the consulate. Bria looked at the papers in her hand and dialed the number on the page. Every minute she sat on hold made her more nervous. Finally, she got an answer. After five minutes of back and forth, she teared at the news: four hundred dollars and at least thirty days. She needed plan B.

Bria thought about the small safe. Theirs was locked and immoveable. She'd have to look for clues to the number they chose. Maybe there was a clue somewhere? Bria started rummaging through the carry-on bags. Finally, she found a small makeup bag. In it was a business card from an oil change, and on the back, a four-digit pin. "Bingo!"

Bria opened the safe and took one hundred dollars in cash. She couldn't take more, could she? She saw their tickets and passports. No, it looked nothing like her. "Damn, Bria, what are you thinking?" She wrote down their names and address, so she could mail them the hundred dollars she borrowed at a later date. It was then that she knew what she'd do. She grabbed the locked iPad she had found in one of their carry-ons. The pin worked!

Bria carefully returned everything to normal and slipped back into her room. It was there that she put the iPad into airplane mode after she was done searching for a solution to her problem.

Bria's mind went from finding a fifty dollar a month room to hitching a ride to the private airstrip and convincing someone to fly her home. Considering she just had to steal the first month's rent, she decided it was time to surround herself with a better quality of people. Tonight, she would have to take Bar

Bingo to the next level.

Bria grabbed her Cushnie Et Ochs dress from the closet and got ready.

A CARNE DI LUPO,
Zanne di Cane.

Devon was coming up empty. His date with an overly excited HR manager was painful. She giggled throughout the entire dinner and failed to present any evidence that she could hold a conversation, let alone any sort of plot to undermine Blooming Sands. Every other sentence was, "Oh my God, that's so interesting!" or "You're so smart!" Although the adulation was appreciated, Devon knew pretty quickly she wasn't going to be the source of any leads. He was thrilled to have to take the late shift at the beach bar so he could leave the date early.

Bria tried to put aside her thievery. "I'll give it back before they leave, I'm just borrowing it," she convinced herself.

She looked damn good. Her power was restored, she now had one hundred and thirty-eight dollars in her purse, and she hoped to come home with even more. Blooming Sands was a short walk up the beach. She'd play a little bar bingo and hopefully find a compassionate soul to help her find her way home.

Bria started walking. The sand was much cooler at night and the warm breeze caressed her skin luxuriously. She almost forgot about the past week and her list of losses. She was a Brigante, she would be fine. *A chi vuole, non mancano modi.* Bria definitely had the will.

The Blooming Sands bar was remarkably empty. Bria was shocked. Thankfully, two men sat alone at the bar. Both seemed like solid prospects, but she opted to sit closer to the man without the wedding ring. Hopefully the after-dinner crowd would make their way out and the groups of golfers would soon find the ocean breeze as alluring as Bria was right now. As she approached the single patron, she studied him for clues: He was single, and most likely here on a work function. He looked as though he was meeting someone as he kept checking his phone. No screensaver, so probably no kids. His casual clothes were professionally cleaned so no live-in. Ahh, a class ring at his age— always a sign of a man who came from nothing and is proud of what he's achieved. He's probably using the alumni network to build his business. In sales, definitely sales. Big sales, some kind of a hot shot. Bria was ready.

"Is that a Harvard ring?"

"Why, yes. Did you attend?"

"I could only be so lucky. I'm a UPenn girl, had to go for second best."

"Well, I wouldn't say that's a bad second. Let me get you a drink. What are you having?"

"Oh, I couldn't."

"I insist, anything."

"A Brooklyn, with Macallan if you don't mind?"

Devon's head spun around.

"Bartender, could you…" the Harvard alumni started.

"Yes, of course. A Brooklyn. Eighteen or twenty-five, miss?" Devon said coldly. He didn't know why he was responding to this stranger like this. The seductress, he thought. "Of all the gin joints," he accidentally said out loud.

"I'm sorry?" Bria asked quizzically. "Do I know you?"

Harvard couldn't help notice the interaction but would never lose a sale, "Twenty-five," he responded for her. He was not going to be outdone by a bartender.

Bria felt something undo her but wasn't sure what. She could not focus on a bartender right now. At the end of the night she would have three days before her flight home. Bria looked at Harvard and smiled coyly, "Thank you."

Devon made the Brooklyn expertly, which he knew didn't go unnoticed. He even played into her game by suggesting to her victim that he refill her glass. Devon would be shocked to see her pull out a wallet, but she didn't. He now had a front-row seat to the seductress in action.

"I put it on his tab," Devon responded. He wanted to keep her there.

Despite his unexplained anger, he couldn't stop noticing how her skin now looked sun-kissed and the red dress she wore accentuated every curve. More so, her dress seemed a beacon calling the moon. Why, Devon wondered, did this woman who was clearly wearing a dress worth thousands, work so hard to get free drinks? You could always see these women coming, especially in his usual crowds. They studied the *Robb Report,* but they dressed discount. Not this one.

Devon's mind couldn't stop. What are the chances the man with the pinky ring and fat fingers was still watching her?

"Bartender, I'll take a martini, Martin Miller, dry, two olives."

Devon was knocked out of his haze. "Martin Miller, dry, two olives coming up!"

"What do you have for white wine?" a couple next to the man asked.

Devon couldn't help but notice the bar filling up. For the first time since he arrived, he had more than two guests at a time. It's amazing what a beautiful woman can do for a place.

"Sancerre? Chardonnay? Give me one moment and I'll show you what I recommend." Devon was good at this.

"No, go away! We don't want any!"

"I have beautiful paintings for you, nice price."

Devon could hear the aggravation of his guests. He remembered the advice and shouted, "Hey! Get off the property!" At that, a half dozen vendors moved beyond a short rail and continued to work for his patrons' attention. Several patrons start to leave the bar and headed back to the resort, but the crowd of beach vendors remained.

It was then that he'd see something he knew he'd never forget.

Bria was furious. She and other patrons asked the bartender to get rid of the unruly group only to receive the response, "Because no one owns the beach in the Dominican, we can only keep them behind the railing. I called security, but it sounds like they know the rules."

Bria was quickly losing her free drink crowd and decided to head back to her hotel. Upon stepping on the sand, two vendors who had been particularly rude to Bria grabbed her arms to stop her. Two female vendors watched and laughed.

"You asking for trouble, white lady. You should know better to dress like a ho-ho," they sang and giggled as the men became more aggressive.

Bria tried to ignore them, and get past them, but a third man joined the other two. The third man, encouraged by the audience of heckling women, grabbed at Bria's breast. Bria's instincts kicked in. She grabbed the man's arm from her breast and pulled him in quickly, catching him off guard. She kneed him with all her might, directly in the groin. He fell to the ground in pain. This seemed to enrage the other two men. One went to grab her arms behind her back as the other approached. She lifted her body up swiftly, used her captor as a brace, and kicked the oncoming man in the face with both heels. As she fell on top of the man behind her, another man from the crowd moved toward her. A hand moved toward her neck from behind and she bit it with all of her might. She sprang up in enough time to use a Jiu jitsu kick to bring him to his knees. The men were enraged and embarrassed in front of the women. She elbowed the man with the bloody arm in the face and started to move toward the first man, who was just then rising to his feet. He put his hands up in a truce as another man tried to attack her from the back. She flipped him over to the sand doing no harm, then stepped forward and kicked him in the groin. She needed to debilitate these men if she wanted to get away. She felt someone come up behind her again, only to be welcomed in the nose with her sharp elbow.

She heard him yell, "No!" and realized it was the bartender.

The gallery of vendors was silent except for gasps of disbelief. Now Bria stood in the middle of the army of peddlers, with only the bartender next to her, nursing his bloodied nose. She couldn't believe what she had just done. In her head, she heard a hawk cry. She slipped her shoes off and walked away from the scene, heading back toward her hotel.

Devon could not believe what had just happened. On top of that, his nose may never be the same. Turns out, the seductress should have been wearing a cape. He couldn't wait to grab a cold beer tonight. Joining his co-workers after his shift around a bonfire had become one of his favorite parts of the job. Tonight, he needed it.

Devin closed the bar and grabbed a bag of cold beers from the ice. As he walked up on his usual group, he found the size had doubled. Everyone was talking about the "sexy tsunami."

"Awe, mon, dis woman, she was so fine. She was wearing a red dress that said fuck me, baby. She had it coming, mon." the pool attendant said, "but she showed dem all right."

Devon shook his head as he entered the circle. He opened a beer and held another up for any takers. "She was fierce."

"You should know, brotah!" At that, the group became riotous. Devon put his cold beer next to his nose until the laughter died.

"Yea, she got me, all right. I was trying to help her."

"She needed no help, brotah. She took those boys down!"

The fire burned early into the morning. Devon could barely keep his eyes open and was about to leave when the conversation about beach trolls started.

"Beach trolls?" asked Devon. "Yeah, yeah, like the Sexy Tsunami. You know, they drink too much, party too much, fuck too much… and are always out for a free drink."

"You pour the drinks, right brothah? He cool?" The man speaking looks around the circle for affirmation. Devon's co-workers nod.

"You know, man. We've got to make a living. These trolls, we just make them pay a little for those drinks they're always scoring. Bad tippers, too. We're just getting what's ours, man." The man tells about a scam he pulled at his resort this week. They bragged about hitting two rooms and cleaning them out during the past week. "They drink too much and they go home with some dude, or they go for a walk in the morning to take care of their hangover, and me and my ladies get to work. I got a guy who comes to the island once a month to buy the passports and licenses for the big dollars. I share any cash and credit cards with my ladies that help me secure the merchandise."

Devon can't believe what he's hearing. Could this be going on at Blooming Sands? Still, not what he needs but he's getting closer to being trusted. He's close. It was worth the elbow to the face to gain this group's trust.

THREE DAYS LEFT

After the episode at Blooming Sands, Bria decided to join the party at the Resort Caribe. The weekly luau was hosted on the concrete patio surrounding the pool. The plastic floats were replaced with floating flames and the buffet was moved outside with a fake plastic roasted pig at the center of the table. Ham and pork products were arranged artistically around the pig and employees handed out leis and encouraged dancing and limbo contests. Bria watched from a small table as she drank tall, bottom-shelf piña coladas. She snacked on cold satay with a side of what tasted like thinned peanut butter rather than the peanut sauce it was pretending to be. With a slight buzz and a full stomach, Bria finally made it to her room around midnight. "It's midnight," she thought, "only three days left."

Bria nursed yet another hangover at breakfast. This time she accompanied it with aches and pains that she had never before felt.

"Do you know what a Bloody Mary is?" she asked the waiter.

Bria sat silently looking at the happy young couples and groups of friends littering the outdoor patio. Bria couldn't help but think of the mess she had made of her life. On top of everything, she knocked out the bartender at the only place in Punta Cana where she could possibly find someone to help her. She had run up and down the beach several times during the past week. This wasn't a strip of luxury resorts. Of course, there were some beautiful time shares, but the Blooming Sands was different. People came for the weather, surely. But as she had learned the night before, the real reason they came was because

Blooming Sands hosted one of the world's most challenging and picturesque golf courses in the world. She knew she would have to go back and apologize.

Bria finished breakfast and headed toward the beach. Finding a place to sleep was overwhelming. She had three days and one hundred and thirty-eight dollars. She thought about how she would survive on her walk to Blooming Sands.

She could rent a room, sneak into the different resorts and eat, maybe braid hair? She thought about what crafts she could sell. Nothing, she thought sadly. Could she hostess at one of the hotels? Maybe that was an option. She'd have to find someone who would pay her cash, she assumed. Bria continued to depress herself as she walked. Something was different on this walk. It was quiet. Not one person had approached her to buy anything. Bria kept walking, enjoying the peace.

As she looked toward the light blue sea, she had to squint as the bright morning sun was no match for her Saint Laurents. As she stared ahead, she noticed a man running by her. Did he have a scarf around his waist? She tried to make out the runner. Was it the naked man from the beach? The thief? Bria started running after him, "Hey! Stop! Hey!" So, he did.

"Why did you stop?" Bria surprised herself with the question.

"Why wouldn't I, Bella? It is not every day that a beautiful woman chases me down the beach." He tried to play her.

"Do you remember me? Where are my things?!? Where is my passport? How dare you! What is this, some kind of cruel joke? Why? Why did you stop running?" Bria asked questions until she lost her breath.

"Bella, Bella, Bella. Nooo. What are you saying?"

"I don't even know your name."

"Bria, Bella, I am Antonio." The formally naked man bowed poetically.

"Of course, you are," Bria paused, "You remembered my name?"

"Of course, Bella. You are so lovely, but you live in New York, and I live right here right now." Antonio seemed so practical in his explanation.

Bella regained her composure, "What about my things, Antonio? What have you done with my money and passport?"

"Your money? I don't need your money, Bella. What happened to your money and your passport? Were they stolen?"

For some reason, Bria trusted this man. She knew he didn't steal her things. This crazy, impetuous, unabashed, Italian gigolo with a lust for life had not stolen her money. She remembered the housekeeper's response and her phone call after she left.

"I'll find it for you," Antonio continued, "Where did you leave them?"

Bria's face relaxed. Why had she relaxed? Because he didn't run? "Bria, you might be a fool," she said to herself out loud.

"No Bella, you are not a fool."

Bria and Antonio walked past the Blooming Sands and talked about the past three days. Before she could mention last night, Antonio stopped. "Do you notice this, Bella?"

"Notice what?" Bria asked.

"No sand fleas."

"Sand fleas?"

"You know," continued Antonio, "those people with the pictures and the braiding. *It's a good price, señor.* Sand fleas!"

Bria laughed. "I'm sure they're just busy harassing someone else."

"No, Bella. Guarda!" Antonio pointed at the beach vendors watching them. They were standing as far as possible from Bria, watching her. "They're watching you, Bella!"

"Nooo..." Bria watched. She took a few steps toward three vendors lined up in front of a resort wall. They scurried in different directions. Bria started walking in the direction of another group in the distance. One man held up his hands and shook his head.

They laughed as she shared the story of last night.

"No!" Antonio said. "You? All those men?" His surprise seemed feigned.

Bria didn't know why she felt so comfortable with Antonio. Maybe because he was Italian? Maybe because he reminded her of her father when he called her "Bella." Maybe, thought Bria, it was just nice not to be alone. They walked down the beach together as the sun rose and the sand warmed.

"Café?" Bria offered.

"Perfetto."

"My place? It's free?" They both laughed as they walked back to Resort Caribe.

REPARATION

After breakfast Bria started her walk back to Blooming Sands. Antonio was a nice distraction from her problems. She planned to ask him for help finding a place to live next time they met. Antonio promised to return in the evening for free dinner. For Bria, it was nice to have plans, and it was even nicer to be able to be honest.

As Bria walked toward the entrance of Blooming Sands, she noticed how the beach vendors moved from her path. She giggled, saying to herself, "It is a nice change."

The bar from the night before was barren. A lonely bartender was rearranging glassware while the beach waiter stayed at his usual post, manning the empty cabanas. In front of his bosses, Bria was sure he would have asked her to enjoy a cocktail in one of the cabanas, but without an audience, futility would not be entertained. Bria made her way past the busy pool and coconut oil toward the elegant building beyond. Although her focus was on apologizing to their employee, Bria walked slowly so she could bask in the opulence surrounding her.

She walked passed the pool bar, hoping to find her good Samaritan. Not him. She stepped up to the well-appointed dining area. She was amazed by the change in temperature. The potted plants and artistic silk awnings created the perfect dining experience. She wondered how the ocean breeze and sweet smell of flowers were perfectly tempered in this beautiful space. Bria followed the sound of Thelonious Monk to the lobby. A young girl in a uniform approached her with a silver tray and tongs, "Warm or cool towel, madam?" She would have paid a fifty-dollar cover charge in any New York club to hear this caliber jazz. She wanted to move into the Blooming Sands lobby. She wondered if they'd notice.

Bria smiled warmly as she walked up to the grand front desk.

"Hi, I had an incident at your hotel last night—" Bria started.

"Oh my!" replied the young girl. "Are you okay? Let me get someone for you." Bria tried to slow her down but there was no stopping her.

At that, the young girl immediately picked up the phone and started talking. "Maria, the woman from last night is here." She said nothing else and hung up abruptly. Bria's mind could not grasp what was happening. She tried to stop the whirlwind of activity that was triggered.

"Yolanda," the young woman's finger rose, "beverages for our guest."

"No, no, you don't understand…" Bria interrupted.

"We are so sorry, madam. Our manager will be out here immediately. May I get you something?"

"No, I just came to apologize."

"Apologize? Oh no! You are a hero," said the girl as she grabbed Bria's hand and guided her to a sofa in the lobby.

"How is your bartender?" asked Bria, afraid to know.

"Oh, Devon? He is strong. He is fine." At that an entourage of suited and uniformed personnel rushed into the lobby and paused. They spotted the two women on the sofa and quickly dismissed the young girl.

"Thank you, Isabella."

"Miss, I'm sorry, we don't even know your name," the man in the suit started.

"Bria. Bria Brigante."

"Miss Brigante, we want to apologize for what happened here last night. Ever since our government allowed residents to sell wares without a license, our beach has been corrupted by, by these vagrants. What you did last night, well…"

Now it was Bria's turn to interrupt, "I'm so sorry. I didn't mean to punch your bartender. I know he was trying to help."

Laughter erupted.

"Miss Brigante, would you allow us to show you something?" Bria had been toying with the idea of offering her marketing services. This was exactly the clientele of whom she was accustomed to catering. But somehow, well, something out of her control was about to happen.

"Of course," Bria hesitated.

The men rose and motioned for her to follow them. She couldn't imagine that she wouldn't be safe in this environment, but what did they want? She followed them from the lobby to an elevator she didn't know existed. The men flanked her quietly as they entered a key in the elevator wall and pushed the button labeled "S." She felt the elevator move down a floor. They emerged to a long hallway with numerous numbered doors. She followed the men to the door marked "Security."

"Why could they possibly be bringing her here?" Bria's hands started to prepare. One thing she had learned at Resort Caribe was that security was useless, and maybe even corrupt. In the Dominican, tourism rules over justice. Had she upset the tourists? She hadn't done anything wrong, had she?

"Have a seat, Miss Brigante. We want to show you something." Bria obliged as she was directed to a chair that faced a wall of cameras.

"Okay, Hector, go ahead."

Hector, who was apparently stationed in this cement cube, lit each screen up with pictures of the beach.

"Miss Brigante, do you notice anything?" In each frame the camera followed Bria as she walked on the beach that morning alone, then with Antonio. Another frame had her walking toward the entrance of Blooming Sands, then toward the pool. In the video, Bria could clearly see what Antonio had noticed himself. The vendors were afraid of her.

"Are you referring to the vendors?"

"Yes, Miss Brigante. Now look at this." The screens changed to up close face shots of each vendor.

"Do you recognize any of them?"

"No, I'm sorry, I don't," Bria obliged.

"Exactly!" the manager exclaimed. He handed her a piece of paper with eight headshots. "These are the vendors who created problems for you last night. None of them is on the beach yet today. But notice the looks you're getting? The beach vendors are afraid of you, Miss Brigante. Word has spread."

Puzzled, Bria asked, "I'm not sure I understand? Why is this important to me? I should be pleased, right? These vendors are a nuisance."

The manager explained how the beach vendors have hurt their reputation. They've been looking for a solution but now headquarters is nervous because sales are down exponentially. They don't want to admit that they can't protect their own guests, but their hands are tied by the law.

"But, Miss Brigante, your hands are not tied by our laws."

Bria sat up. Are they offering her a job in security? "What are you saying?"

"Miss Brigante, all you have to do is sit on our beach and these vagrants will not come near."

"For today, at least." Bria surprised herself with her response. They could be offering her a solution to a more pressing dilemma and she was trying to talk them out of it? Bria caught herself and went quiet.

"Islanders have long memories, Miss Brigante. My grandmother was born in the Dominican. She used to always say, '*Recuerda al toro para que nunca más tengas que vivir el dolor.*' It means, remember the bull so you don't have to relive the pain. Trust me, Miss Brigante. You were a bull that they never saw coming."

Bria thought of her father's journal.

"So how can I help?" Bria asked.

LOST GIRL FOUND

"Devon, your attacker was here this morning," sang the HR manager when she saw him. "Last night was wonderful, by the way."

"Oh really. What was she doing here?"

"She's still here," whispered last night's date.

"Really? Where is she?" Devon couldn't help himself.

"She's downstairs with Señor Alavarez."

"That's curious," Devon responded.

"You know what's curious, is I think that's the same girl that man with the picture was looking for. He said it is his daughter. Maybe I should tell him?" Devon's interest piqued more.

"What man with the picture?"

"Mr. Smith. He's in room 1219. He's always hanging out at your bar. Shorter guy, stocky, light brown hair with extra gel—what's left of it..." she rambled.

"Does he have a pinky ring and a thick gold chain around his neck?" Devon asked.

"Yes! Yes! That's him. He was offering a few of us a hundred dollars if we could tell him where she was. Maybe I'll tell him. We could use it for our next date!"

Devon almost choked on his next sentence. "Hold on, who does he say she is again?"

"His daughter. I guess he's trying to make amends, hasn't seen her in years."

Devon thought of the first time he saw them at the airport. "Mr. Smith." He was sure that was not his real name. He was in disguise, but not a full disguise. He was answering to someone on the phone. Why would he be telling someone about the seductress on the phone if he was her father. The story was not making sense. Why wouldn't he have approached her right there? Why would he go to all the effort of following her here?

"Hey, beautiful," Devon responded. The HR manager blushed. "I'll pay for the next date but, do me a favor?"

"Of course."

"Something doesn't sound right about his story. Can you keep this a secret until I dig around and find out a little more? If he's up to no good, we could be putting her in danger."

"Oooo… You're so smart Devon! Imagine that? In our hotel? It's like the movies."

As last night's date continued to gush, Devon committed Mr. Smith's room number to memory and decided to do a little snooping.

"Where's Mr. Smith now?" Devon asked.

"I think I saw him walking toward the beach a little while ago," she responded.

"Ping me when he comes back, can you? I'm going to start a casual conversation with him. Maybe I can learn more."

"Of course, handsome!" Devon winced hearing those words come from her.

Devon knew he was onto something greater. What are the chances that a creepy Italian guy is looking for a man-killing seductress who just happens to be in the private company of the hotel manager? There is definitely some connection between the three. Devon was almost running to his room when the door to the security room opened. As he passed, Bria Brigante stepped out of the security office, right into his path.

"Oh, it's you! You're the reason I came today. I'm so sorry, I thought you were attacking me. I am so sorry I hit you in the nose."

Devon, for the first time, was at a loss for words. Five men stood around the tall, beautiful man-eater.

"I'm Bria, Bria Brigante." She extended her hand, "How are you doing?"

Composing himself, Devon looked at her company, "I'm fine, thank you." Devon was working hard to keep his pride in check. What was it about this woman? He wanted to kiss her and run from her at the same time.

"Devon, Miss Brigante is going to be working with Blooming Sands down by your bar. I think she's proven that she doesn't need your help—" Chortles and jeers from the group of men made it difficult for the manager to finish his sentence, "but you'll show her around tomorrow, won't you?"

"Of course, Mr. Alvarez."

"That would be lovely, Devon. Thank you," Bria added with sly smile.

Devon was furious. This stroke of luck, having to cozy up to someone who is obviously up to no good, should have him soaring. Instead, he is writhing with anger. She made a fool out of him. He was going to take her down. He finished his race to his room. Hopefully Mr. Smith was still at the beach. He ran in, grabbed the master key that Max had given him, and moved to room 1219 as fast as he could, avoiding suspicion.

"Housekeeping!" Devon knocked. He opened the door a crack, "Housekeeping!"

Devon entered the room and looked around. A travel kit bought in the lobby sat in the bathroom. Besides that, the room was sparse. He opened the closet door to find a pair of pants and the familiar leather coat. He rummaged through the pockets looking for a clue. He found a set of keys to a Lincoln on a New York Yankees key chain. A few other unidentifiable keys were also on the ring. On the valet was an empty Tommy Bahama bag. He opened the bag and found a receipt for a couple shirts, underwear and a pair of shorts. The hotel laundry bag was missing, presumably holding the missing shirt downstairs. Nothing else. There were no suitcases. Not even a small carry-on.

Devon walked next to the bed and found a small hotel note pad. He grabbed the top blank page and put it safely in his shirt pocket. He stepped out to the balcony where he found a view of the pool and the remnants of an old cigar and a glass that smelled of bad scotch. The chair was positioned facing the pool and Devon imagined him sitting here for hours watching for, who he assumed could only be, Bria Brigante. But why? As Devon walked back in the room, he noticed a small case wedged behind the Blooming Sands signature planter. He reached back, pulled out the case, and opened it. The only thing he found was black foam with the indentation of a hand gun. Dylan Lancaster was an avid collector and would regularly bring his three boys hunting and skeet shooting. Devon wished he had paid more attention now. He could only guess that the box held a .22, but he couldn't be sure. Devon slid the case back behind the planter exactly as he had found it. One last scan of the room and Devon left, the adrenaline coating his back.

"How did Mr. Smith get a gun from Newark to the Dominican?" Devon wondered. "More importantly, why does he need a gun at the Blooming Sands Resort?"

Devon unfolded the small piece of paper when he got back to his room. He held it up to the light trying to make out what had been written on it previously. It was a mess. He made out the words "Caribe" written several times in a list. He saw larger words, more cryptic written in a different direction over the top. Two notes. All he wanted was a pencil. He looked around the room for something to help him better read the words on the paper.

Each room, although found in the lowest level of the hotel, had a small window at the top of the wall. Outside each window was a small garden. Devon grabbed a washcloth from the bathroom and slid the glass pane open. He reached over the lower sill and wiped the washcloth in the hearty soil. After shaking the dirt off the cloth, he gently grazed the paper with the dirty rag. Words started to appear more clearly. Caribe was written sixteen times, and only the first two were crossed off. Across the top of the list was another list in larger, more hurried print:

2 left
1 right
Bodega/corner
Paolo
Lb of prosciutto

Devon looked at the list. Directions of some sort? Prosciutto in the DR? He'd go check it out anyway. This was all he had. Based on the gun, no matter how he felt about Bria, he couldn't take the risk that she could get hurt. But then again, was she part of this? Max had no idea how right his timing was.

TWO RESORTS LEFT

Vinny left Blooming Sands. He had two more hotels on his list and his boss was getting nervous. The morning's call with a colleague confirmed this.

"This is getting serious, Vegas. How hard can it be to find her? It's a small fuckin island. The boss is not happy. It's been nine fucking years, Vegas."

"Yeah, yeah. I'll get 'er. I should'a grabbed her at the airport."

"That would'a been the end of all of us. Too many cameras. You did the right thing, Vegas. Just find her."

"I got it, I got it."

"Whatta I tell the boss?"

"Tell 'im I'm on it."

Vinny headed back to the Blooming Sands. He had to check on the other gun and grab something to eat. Vinny decided to grab a beer at the swim up bar. He was hot and tired from walking all morning. He stepped into the lobby and walked toward the gift shop. As he threw cash down on the counter to pay for the swim trunks he found, he was greeted by a bubbly mix of nosiness and awkwardness. "Hi, Mr. Smith! Um... are you going for a swim?"

Irritated, he said, "No, I'm going for a beer but this fuckin' place makes you swim to it."

"Hee hee hee... Oh Mr. Smith, you're so funny!"

At that, the bundle of anxious exuberance left.

Vinny walked down the steps to the pool. Despite his

extraordinary amount of hair, the week had darkened his arms and face, leaving his oversized gut gleaming through his hair-covered torso. As he waded through the water toward the bar, he was shocked to feel how much he enjoyed the cool water. It was the first time he had stopped looking and walking in a week. Even in his room, he had perched himself on the balcony where he watched the pool and dining room in hopes of finding her. How could she not show up here? This was her kind of place.

"The coldest beer you got," Vinny barked at the bartender.

"Tough day on vacation, sir?" The bartender answered.

"You could say that. Hey, you got a pretty good gig here." Vinny looked around at all the beautiful people surrounding the bar. In New York, he could get any one of them. Here, nobody knew him. He was suddenly aware of his years of pasta and red wine.

"Good gig? We should get hazard pay here," said the bartender with a laugh. "You hear about last night?" At that, the bar exploded with tales of the tall, dark haired model who knocked out the bartender and six beach vendors. As the story grew, the number of vendors grew to a dozen and the bartender ended up in the hospital.

"Any chance she used jiu jitsu?" Vinny asked.

"That's what you're going to ask? This woman was smoking hot, legs that start at her neck, wearing a killer dress, and takes out a band of sand fleas and all you care about is which martial art she used to do it?"

Vinny ignored his comment, "Long brown hair that looks like it should be in a TV commercial for Pantene or some shit?"

"Yea, yea, that's her. You know her?"

"Son of a bitch." Vinny can't believe what he just heard. "She's right fucking here, right under my fucking nose. Where is she now?"

The bartender was a little put off. Something told him not to answer the question.

"Where the fuck is she now?" Vinny repeats himself.

"Um, dude, I don't think she's staying here. They said she

left and walked down the beach after beating up those guys."

"Which way?" The bartender seemed too rattled to answer.

"Which way did she walk?" Vinny growled.

A new voice answered, "She walked toward the vendor shanties."

MOVING UP

Bria could not believe her luck. She not only negotiated cash payment as a contractor, but a reduced rate if they gave her a room and food. She would live in luxury and sit on the beach while she straightened out her passport. They were even sending a car for her tomorrow to collect her belongings.

She added the manager's quote to the leather-bound journal. She was the bull, she laughed at herself. She thought of her father and realized she was also the good wine. She didn't need to sell herself to the Blooming Sands. They had recognized her value without her needing to pitch her talents. However, it wasn't her marketing talents they were buying.

She showered without care for the first time in several days. Bria grabbed a simple sundress, threw her hair in a soft pile on top of her head, and headed to the beach. It was dusk and Punta Cana was on the eastern side of the island, but Bria still loved sunsets on the beach. She sat in the pure white sand and looked out at the sea. Her mother had taught her to meditate using her senses. In her broken English, she'd say "sensual meditation" and would always be rewarded with Papà's and Bria's giggles.

She thought of her mother as she closed her ears and focused on her nose. She would focus on the first sense, smell. She smelled the calcium and quartz of the sand, the salt of the sea, and the faint smell of hibiscus and earth while the wind blew. She smelled the moist air and how it felt heavier as it moved through her nasal passages. The smell of sunscreen and lotions were gone. She could smell the faint and distant smell of chlorinated water from the pool behind her when the breeze would shift slightly. She smelled a fire far away and something cooking. The warm aroma of a tropical feast. She moved onto visual meditation, the second sense. She watched the waves softening and creating a gentle roll as they crashed on the sand. She watched the water drain from the higher sand, leaving a moving line that chased the surf back into the sea. She saw lovers kissing, still in the water. She saw rows of cabanas and closed umbrellas that dotted the long, expansive sands. She smiled as she saw the "sand fleas" a safe distance from her but watching, while small grains of sand fell from her feet. She looked at the white sand as it complemented her tanned toes and pale polish. As she focused on listening, she heard birds chittering in their foreign tongue and rolling waves roaring despite their calm. Bria heard the peacock's scream. Was he looking for his peahen? She smiled as she knew exactly where the peahen was.

    It was then that Bria realized, as she listened to the peacock scream, that she had been too focused on being a peacock and not being herself. For once, Bria thought about who she is. She didn't think about her losses or the past. She didn't get lost in who Papà wanted her to be or the mistakes she had made. As she tasted the slight saltiness in the air and felt the soft sand between her fingers, she could only think about one thing.

    Who is Bria Brigante?

PING

Devon made sense of the directions he found in Mr. Smith's room. He borrowed a car from the valet and followed the road leading out of Blooming Sands. He had taken his second left, first right and found the bodega on the corner. He was so close to the hotel, so close to immeasurable wealth, yet the community three turns away was devastatingly poor. Cinderblock homes stood crowded with people. They had no windows and the children who played in the dirt streets kicked an old soccer ball barefoot, with tattered clothes. The bodega was white stucco and rounded the corner of the block. On the counter, as if on display for onlookers, stood a mangey dog in a wire cage. Devon wondered if he was for sale to play with or to eat. The white walls had two garage doors, one facing each street, that were drawn up creating an open-air market. The white stucco was occasionally interrupted with a Bud Light or Presidente sign. Two overly tanned grandfathers sat at a small bistro table playing checkers while another stood on the corner of the building drinking a beer. Devon stepped inside and looked for a sign for prosciutto. There was none.

He asked the woman sweeping the floor, "I'm looking for Paolo." She looked at him closer. "Paolo?" he repeated.

"Ah, Paolo. Si, Paolo."

"Donde esta Paolo?" Devon struggled through putting even a simple sentence together in Spanish. Hopefully Paolo spoke English. The old woman put her hand forward, her palm facing out. As she shuffled out the side door, Devon realized he had no plan. Emotion drove him here. Could emotion save him as well? This was no longer about helping a friend. Was this about curiosity? Goodwill? Was Devon seduced by Bria Brigante as easily as her marks? How did Devon Lancaster end up in a bodega on a dirt road in Punta Cana? Devon Lancaster could buy this village and wouldn't need Dylan's help. But right now, Devon Lancaster was risking his life for a woman he didn't even know. He knew that there was no way these two had anything to do with the money lost at Blooming Sands. Why was he trying to connect the two? There was something about Bria Brigante that he needed to know.

At that, however, Devon Lancaster needed to figure out how to get out of this mess alive.

"Who are you?" The man asking was dark skinned and wore American clothes. He was better dressed than the people in the bodega, and he spoke far better English.

"Are you Paolo?" Devon stood firm.

"No. Who are you?"

"I'm here for a pound of prosciutto." Devon mustered his best Italian accent. He could count the times he had prosciutto. On vacation in Sorrento, at the market in Barcelona, at the opening of Mario Batali's restaurant before all that scandal.

"Who sent you?"

"Mr. Smith."

"Gesù Cristo, this guy! Hold on. What's your name?" The man was all business.

"...Dino." Devon hoped the man didn't hear his hesitation. Damn it, Devon. Dean Martin? Is that the only name you could come up with? Devon mentally berated himself for his bad decisions.

"Hold on." The short man walked back outside. The next few minutes would be telling.

Devon's phone pinged. "Mr. Smith is on his way to the swim up bar." Devon regretted his comments to Max about the HR manager earlier that morning. Maybe she would be useful, after all.

The man returned. "Who called you? Let me see your phone."

The message displayed his last message. Thankfully, he had entered last night's date in as HR. He looked at Devon, "Who's H.R.?"

"An associate." Devon was ready for that one.

"OK, you know Mr. Smith, you check out. Here's your package. Tell Mr. Smith we're sorry for the delay. New York is a little backed up." Devon just nodded and grabbed the bag. His legs seemed too weak for his body. He clicked the lock on the hotel's black Suburban and was thankful he grabbed a car without the hotel's name painted on it. Devon put the package on the passenger seat and drove away, trying to hide the rear plate from view of the bodega just in case.

Devon drove toward the hotel and when he got on smooth road again, he opened the bag. It was a simple brown paper grocery bag, rolled four or five times from the top. Inside Devon could feel a hard, heavy case. His mouth grew dry. What had he just done?

Devon threw his things hurriedly on his bed and jumped into his swim trunks. He knew employees weren't allowed at the guests' pool, but he'd have to play stupid. Just as he reached the counter he heard Pinky Ring.

"Which way?" He asked. No one responded.

"Which way did she walk?" Pinky Ring repeated the words slowly.

Devon spoke up, "She walked toward the vendor shanties."

NOW WHAT?

Bria looked around her new room. It was luxurious. Egyptian cotton, bathrobes, divine toiletries, a view of the crystal blue sea. Too bad she had to meet that bartender today because she could just stay and luxuriate in her new room for a week. She remembered this life. This was her life with Mama and Papà. Bria decided to wait until the next day to focus on consulates and passports. This morning, she would lay in bed, order room service, and enjoy the room until she had to meet at three. Bria rolled in cotton sheets remembering the luxury of high thread counts and room service.

Devon opened the bag on his bed. He needed to call Max. He needed to call the police. In the bag was a large handgun, bigger than what he presumed the case held in Mr. Smith's room. A .38? Devon was no gun expert, but he knew by the weight that this was meant to cause damage. He needed to get Mr. Smith out of the resort— away from Bria, away from Blooming Sands, and especially away from Devon. He picked up his phone and tapped Max Bloomfield III's name.

"Max, it's Devon."

The two talked for an hour with Max clicking away, trying to learn more. Twelve nineteen was paid for with cash. This was against company policy. He also didn't have a reservation, affirming Devon's theory that Pinky Ring was following her. These were not the actions of an intentional plot. This explained the empty room and so much more. But, why?

"You can't call the police, Devon. It would be bad press. Especially if we don't have solid evidence." Max nearly pleaded in his tone and Devon stared down at the illegal, molded lead sitting next to him.

"Bria Brigante?" Max asked. "B-R-E-A?"

"I don't know." Devon said.

"B-R-I-A? (pause) Damn, she beautiful! It says she works at Vicci Marketing in New York. She won an award for something a few weeks ago...She's listed as an alumni for Wharton undergrad... Do you remember her at all?"

Devon's conspiratorial thinking kicked in. "Max, maybe she knows you? Maybe she's playing a long game here?"

"I don't see why a smart, Madison Avenue marketing exec would want to risk everything to steal a few million dollars. She can make that herself."

"And why would a guy be following her? Stalkers don't have seedy connections and bosses on the other end of the phone who are in on it." Devon reasoned.

"She is beautiful."

"I know. You should see her in person, Max."

"Hold on, hold on. (pause) Fuck me." There was silence on Max's end.

"What is it?" Devon asked.

Max read:

> "Downtown Manhattan was gridlocked for hours yesterday as reputed crime boss Benedetto Brigante, also known as "Papà", was eulogized at Saint Peter's Roman Catholic Church in New York in a closed casket ceremony. Problems began when the procession that started at the church weaved through Mulberry Street and then toward his home in Short Hills, New Jersey.
>
> A relative who was unable to get inside the church service explained to press this was their family church since the Brigante family came to America. Thousands filled the church while fire fighters and police worked to keep the crowds at bay. Even more well-wishers lined the streets through SoHo, Little

Italy, and Hell's Kitchen neighborhoods as the hearse made its way through town. License plates from Boston, Providence, Chicago and Miami joined the procession — many with tinted windows— making spectators even more curious about Papà Brigante and the extent of his reach in the Mafioso community.

Benedetto Brigante, his wife, their younger daughter and their driver were killed when a car bomb was detonated as they returned from seeing "The Lion King" on Broadway on Friday night. Their oldest daughter was expected to be in the car but escaped death, presumably because of a high school dance.

Benedetto Brigante is survived by his seventeen-year-old daughter, his brother, sister-in-law, and their daughter. Their names are being withheld while the incident is under investigation."

Max paused. "This was nine years ago. Hold old do you think she is?"

The two men were silent. Devon didn't need to answer the question.

"Do you think?" Max asked.

"I don't know, but it makes sense. I'll call the police," said Devon almost solemnly.

"No! You can't call the police. We don't even know if anything is going on. Besides, she is exactly where we want her right now, in your capable hands."

"What? Max, I don't know…"

"Devon, if the mafia is attacking our properties, we need to know. It won't stop at a beautiful vixen with some karate skills," reasoned Max.

"What do I do about this gun?"

"Leave the gun, take the cannolis." Max chuckled at himself.

Devon stayed silent. This was nothing to laugh at. He wondered if his friend knew what he was asking.

IN PLAIN SIGHT

Bria's new job had very few restrictions. She was an independent contractor who was hired to "ensure the security of the Blooming Sands' guests on and off their property." She was offered a branded polo but reminded the security team that she had taken down four men in a two-thousand-dollar dress. It was then, the manager also reminded the team that just having her at the bar drew some of the golfers out to the beach bar, which then in turn attracted a hoard of opportunistic tourists. Bria just being Bria— was also good for business. Bria couldn't help but smile at the manager's marketing prowess. *Al buon vino non bisogna frasca.*

Devon was conflicted by the time he met Bria at the bar. Here was some mafioso princess trying to take advantage of his friend. Had the mafia gotten smarter? Wharton? Was the other night staged? And Pinky Ring, where did he fit in? Devon still couldn't bear to call him Mr. Smith. He knew it was a cover, and a bad one at that. What if he was trying to kill Bria? How would he stay close enough to find out what was happening but far enough away to stay safe? Max's favor just seemed to be the biggest of his life.

"Hi, I'm Devon Lanc—just call me Devon."

"Bria. Pleased to meet you again, Devon." Bria was used to men acting strange around her. She was surprised by how handsome Dylan Lanc-whatever was. His blonde hair was well cut, not your typical island cut. He was tan, but the slight red tint on his skin and the smell of sunscreen told of someone who had only arrived a week or so ago. She couldn't get over his hair cut. That was an expensive cut and reminded her of the boys at Wharton. Bria looked for other clues, but Devon seemed something of a contradiction. He didn't seem as though he belonged here. His grammar was far too refined. He was definitely a WASP, but what was he doing here? His piercing blue eyes seemed to always be somewhere else. It wasn't sexual, just slightly absent, as though he was always trying to figure something out or deep in thought. What she did know, was Devon Lanc was pretending to be someone he wasn't. Why had he said, "Of all the gin joints?" Did he know her? Something about Devon didn't sit well. He came from money, was new here, a former frat boy, but played a poor bartender living in the basement of the Blooming Sands?

"I'm glad to see your nose is no worse for wear after the other night."

"The manager made a mistake when he suggested I put your drinks on the hotel expense sheet. He has no idea what you drink. A few people might be offended that you ruin good whiskey with cherries and bitters."

"Have you ever had one?"

He blushed and said, "Yes. Fifteen— love, your serve."

Bria smiled slyly, "Hmm."

This woman got under Devon's skin. He watched her look him up and down, assessing him. He was not one of her pawns at the bar. He could feel the heat rise inside of him. The nose comment, he knew what that was. She was trying to put Devon Lancaster in his place, beneath her. He was glad he didn't mention his last name. If this was a ploy to take down Max, and she went to Wharton, she'd surely know the Lancaster name. People like her did their homework.

There was not much to show her as it turns out. His date from the other night walked Bria through the employee areas and gave her a locker, "even though she was officially not an employee but a contractor." Fitting, Devon thought. It also limited the access Max would have to her information.

Devon walked behind the bar while Bria stood near the rail that had been previously filled with beach vendors. As he made a Brooklyn the way she liked it—two cherries and Macallan twenty-five— Devon decided he would play this a little differently. Bria Brigante was the master of seduction. He had witnessed it first-hand. The other night, men were lining up to buy her a hundred-dollar cocktail. If he wanted to learn about the real Bria Brigante, he needed to be someone she has never seen before. He needed to be... unaffected.

Devon took the Brooklyn and put it down on the bar. As Bria looked out to the beach, Devon kept his voice dry, "Your drink." He turned away before she could see him looking at her and started organizing the bar. He felt her step toward the bar and stare at him slightly longer than she should. Two could play this game, he thought.

Bria grabbed her drink. "What is up with this guy?" she thought as she watched Devon ignore her. Deciding she had no time for him, she grabbed her drink and walked down to the lone waiter standing under a palm tree, still hoping for guests.

"I'm Bria." She extended her hand and smiled warmly. His eyes shone of shock and awe that this beautiful woman was talking to him.

"Don't you get tired of standing here waiting for customers?" she asked.

"Yes, madam. But I have to wait on this section until there is an opening at the resort's main restaurants. Until then, I will entertain the palms." Bria chuckled.

"Well, what would you say if I could fill all these chairs and cabanas for you?"

"Well, madam, I might give you my first born so that I might feed my other five!" His eyes brightened with laughter.

"Well, let me see what I can do. But I need a small favor in order to make it happen."

Bria suggested the waiter tell the beach vendors that Bria

was now working here as a contractor and she wasn't an employee of the hotel. This meant she could do whatever she wanted. "Let them know there are more of me. They know me now, but we don't want them thinking it's only me. They'll be back every time I use the bathroom."

In return, Bria committed to sitting on his chairs and encouraging the afternoon crowd to dine on the beach under the incredible chandeliered cabanas. She assured him she had a way with men. The waiter blushed.

"Oh yes, madam, I see that."

"Please, it's Bria."

"OK, Miss Bria. Thank you, Miss Bria."

Bria smiled as she noticed the sand fleas walking swiftly, as close to the water's edge as they could, as they passed in front of Blooming Sands. She walked toward them and they sped up. *"What a job!"* she thought. Bria wanted to pinch herself. This wasn't a job she could live on indefinitely, but right now, she had her necessities covered and a little extra to cover the costs of her passport.

Damn! Devon thought. She's been here thirty minutes and already every seat was filled at the bar. Devon was too busy to add up the business she was generating but would do that at the end of his shift.

"Marketing," he scoffed. "She's a marketer all right. Sex sells."

UNDER HIS NOSE

Vinny couldn't believe his eyes.

As he walked back to his hotel, there she was. Bria Brigante was standing on the sand talking to a waiter. He had walked twenty miles of sand and drank gallons of rum punch at sixteen different hotels. On the last day, she shows up at his hotel. Not one of the hotels with the name Caribe in them, she showed up at the Blooming Sands. At the last hotel on his list, he lost a couple hundred dollars only to find out she left the hotel this morning. Now, she was standing in the sand talking to a waiter right in front of his hotel.

She looked as beautiful as her mother. He could understand why Papà brought her mother home with him to America after just meeting her. She was mesmerizing, and her daughter wasn't far behind. Looks were the only thing she had in common with her mother. Since his boss saw her at the Plaza getting into a car, he had learned that Bria Brigante was nothing like her sweet Italian mother. She was all Papà Brigante, and that mixture was lethal.

Bria Brigante was wiped off the map after her family's accident. For a while, Vinny tracked her to her uncle's house, but she was under heavy security there. Between the Brigante family and the police, there was no touching her. When Papà's brother was helped off the side of the bridge, there was a young woman in the car. For years the families thought she was in the car, until last month when Vinny's boss saw her at the Plaza. Seeing her now, Vinny understood why he was so sure it was her. Vinny's boss followed the car to the Upper West Side where she entered a brownstone with her boyfriend, or so he thought. By the time Vinny got there, Bria had disappeared. A couple weeks later, she showed up at *The Meet*, and here he was. After paying off almost fifty bouncers and hosts at the most exclusive Manhattan night clubs, it finally paid off. Tonight, he would not let her slip away.

Vinny made his way to the beach bar, where he had camped his first two days in Punta Cana, sure she would materialize. She hadn't. Now, the bar was filling up quickly and the bartender seemed new. "Could be a long wait," thought Vinny, sitting as far from the beach as he could while still seeing it.

He watched Bria walk around the beach, "What the hell is she doing?" He noticed the bartender watching her as well. Damn, he thought. This woman will be hard to get alone, there are always eyes on her. He picked up his phone.

"Boss, I got eyes on her. Just a matter of finding the right time now."

In the short time Vinny was on the phone, the bar filled. He was never going to get a fucking drink. He wondered if Bria would recognize him. She was a child when he saw her last. She was sitting on the grand staircase while he was sweating, waiting for her father. He tried to have a conversation with her but the only thing he could think of was, "Would she hear the gun Papà capped him with through the office door?" He was relieved when Bria was invited in and Papà had her pour some of his "special wine." You could tell Papà adored her. Vinny remembered taking the wine hesitantly thinking, "He would never let this child see a man die in front of her."

What he learned about Bria in the last month since she resurfaced was as far from her mother as he could have imagined. She lived a destructive lifestyle and was never alone. There had been dozens of near meetings but by the time Vinny got the call, she was drunk and had just left with someone. Vinny had been following her since her appearance at *The Meet.* The timing was never right and the security in her building was too tight for a one-man job.

It would be tonight. She would inevitably be alone. All he had to do was wait.

GOOD FOR BUSINESS

Devon watched Bria work the crowd. The entire night, the bar stayed busy. The hotel manager, thankfully, had seen the crowd from the pool and sent backup. Devon took the front half of the bar so he could keep an eye on Bria. By the end of his shift, he had tallied over twenty-four thousand dollars in sales and almost two hundred additional customers over his six-hour shift.

"How did this happen?" Max couldn't help but sound incredulous.

"I can't believe we didn't see this sooner. Bria Brigante did. She knew exactly what to do."

"Devon, has the shark been baited?" Max asked.

"What? Oh, am I being blinded by her beauty? Ha! No, man. Sex sells, though."

Devon explained how the vendors being afraid of Bria kept the customers at the bar. Then he explained how she would fill the beach.

"She'd point out how romantic the moonlight was while lounging in a cabana. The honeymooners loved it, I even saw her talking to a few couples walking by. She made it look easy. After filling the cabanas, she'd walk the beach and those damn sand fleas would scramble in the other direction. She's a natural, Max. The golfers come to the bar when they see her, they buy good scotch and top shelf drinks. Then beautiful women start showing up from the beach because they see a bunch of rich guys hanging out alone at the nicest bar on the beach and next thing you know, Blooming Sands is the place to be. The guys love the attention and are all wound up from Bria, so they shoot for second best. She keeps them engaged until the women show up. Then she plants all these seeds when they hook up about the cabanas. The guy down there is finally making some money tonight. I don't know what the food take last night was, but I've never seen so many oysters and shrimp delivered to the beach. I had to call Jesse to bring down extra cases of Champagne and ice buckets."

"That's unbelievable." Max was stunned. "How did we miss this?"

Devon explained. "It didn't align. It wasn't an even drop across the board. Reservations were down but the reviews about the hotel were terrific. I bet if we look, it's repeat business and word of mouth. The island's recession changed the laws so now residents don't need permits to sell to tourists. It probably took six months for the law to have a full effect."

"Good job, man! Looks like it's time to send the copter. We have some celebrating to do!" Max exclaimed.

"No, no. Give me a few days, there's one more mystery I need to solve."

STAKEOUT

Vinny sat at the crowded bar hidden behind the bottles for hours. The bar stayed busy right until the end and Bria stayed busy walking back and forth from the beach to the bar. She was talking and laughing, and Vinny sat getting drunker and drunker.

"Coffee, please."

When the bartender brought his coffee, Vinny asked about Bria. "The girl, what's her story?"

"Yeah, Bria. I guess she kicked some vendors' asses the other night and they hired her to control the beach vendors and scare them away. Funny, huh?" The bartender ogled Bria as he talked about her.

"She stayin' here?" Vinny asked.

"Yeah, good gig, right? We'll see how long they stay afraid of her. Can't imagine it will be that long. Seems like she's good for business though."

"Thanks." Vinny threw his room key on the bar to pay the bill. After signing for his drinks, he moved to a lounge chair by the pool. He could just see the beach but figured he was safe because Bria would have to walk by him to get to her room.

THE JOB

Bria woke the next morning. The sun was beaming through the curtains and her arms felt strapped to her side. She tried to roll over, but the sheets held her captive. Why were they so tight? Bria's heart raced as she tried to free herself from the tangled mess of linen.

She should have had a great sleep; she was finally comfortable and had a plan to get home. But no, she woke to the reality that she still had overwhelming bills, maxed out credit cards, and no advertising agency in the tri-state area would touch her with a ten-foot pole. Worse even, she had lost her best and only friend.

Bria picked up the stolen iPad that laid next to her. She removed the SIM card and connected to the hotel's wi-fi so she could check her emails. More of the same. Turndowns and angry co-workers, clients and wives. Did it matter anymore who sent it? The Brigante in her couldn't help but want revenge. But revenge wouldn't get Julia back. What really mattered was Julia, and Julia had not responded.

Bria could celebrate this small victory, but she could no longer avoid reality. She'd never make enough money to pay for her apartment in the city - let alone the minimums on her credit card bills—being a beach security guard. She had one real pay check left back home that would cover her bills for thirty days until her passport was figured out, but then what? How did she end up here? Just saying her new job title out loud seemed surreal.

Bria changed into her running clothes and decided to go for

a run on the beach to figure out how to get out of this mess.

Bria smiled as she crept by the hairy man sleeping on the lounge chair. He must have passed out there last night. She was surprised she didn't notice him on her way upstairs. She was still flying on her short-term high. Her emotions were erratic. One minute she was being calmed by her beautiful surroundings and ocean breeze, the next she wanted to scream and was praying for her father to be back so she could jump in his arms and cry. As Bria ran, her emotions were on full display for the islanders. Anger, fear, retaliation, loneliness, and sometimes a glimmer of excitement… each emotion took its turn overwhelming her. She welcomed the burn as her legs worked the sand. She ran by the vendor shanties, which were yet to be opened. She loved running in this direction because she would pass a mile of empty beach front and the hotels were more spread out. She had destroyed her reputation in New York, but she had to protect it here. The islanders couldn't see her cry.

Each morning, Bria made it a little further down the beach on her run. She imagined one day running all the way to Santo Domingo. Before she left the Dominican, she promised herself a day's reward and lunch at the sweet provincial outdoor café she saw next to the daffodil colored building.

Today she ran past the Hard Rock Café to the long stretch of undisturbed beachfront. It was here that her emotions cascaded in. Tears streamed down both cheeks as she ran faster, trying to make her legs hurt so she'd forget her other pains: loneliness and fear. She remembered the sensual meditation from her mother. She tried only to focus on what she heard. The waves. They were more aggressive here and you could almost hear how they met from different directions and crashed against each other in the sea. She heard birds. She heard more birds than she could imagine counting, and she heard the wind. She heard the warm breeze through the palms.

As she kept running, she was distracted by the land she noticed jutting out toward the sea with acres of luxury homes being built. At least, she imagined they were luxury homes. She wouldn't stop running. She'd imagine she was successful, right here, and the homes she looked at, well, one was hers. The biggest one with the best ocean views. She imagined drinking coffee from her kitchen with the walls opened up to the sea. The breeze and the soft aroma of flowers caressing her skin. Her gait got faster. As she rounded the property, the beach disappeared into a cliff. She would get to the other side, she decided. As she stepped in the rough surf, the waves slapped her hard into the jagged rocks that she used for safety. The floor of the sea was soft but the rocks were anything but. She didn't stop. She must have been crazy, she thought at one point as her thin body was slammed into the wall of the cliff. In one alcove, the water gurgled like a cauldron and Bria asked herself if she should continue. Her legs, tired from running, burned with their new challenge. As she noticed a small shelf where she could pause and catch her breath, the water's force pulled her under its crushing weight. Bria spun out of control, finally grasping her nose with her fingers as she feared she could no longer hold her breath. The waves pushed her further and further under the sea's belly. The sand beneath her was bright and reflected the morning sun, making it impossible to see which way was up. Bria's body was exhausted and being tossed from one crag to another in the crucifying surf. How would she escape the water's fury?

NEXT ORDER OF BUSINESS

"Oh, shit." Devon could not believe his eyes. In the insanity of last night, he completely forgot about Mr. Smith. There he was. It was seven in the morning and he was mouth-open, head-back, and snoring on the edge of the pool. Did he fall asleep waiting for her? Had he found her? Devon had been sitting in the dining room waiting for Bria to emerge since six. Why had he assumed she was an early riser, he wondered? There was something about Bria Brigante that was overwhelming his senses. Mafia? There was something about her that made this argument completely feasible and something that was missing from that equation. Something was going on with her and it was more than her beauty. She was everything Devon hated, but she was lodged in his brain. The thought of her being a mafia princess made the seductress seem even more inviting, but more dangerous. What was her story? One thing he knew, he needed to keep her safe in order to find out.

Devon tapped on Mr. Smith's shoulder. "Mr. Smith, would you like me to have the hostess bring you a cool cloth to freshen up, sir?"

"What? Who? What do you want? What the fuck?"

Without thinking twice, Devon responded, "Oh, I'm so sorry, Mr. Smith. I thought you wouldn't want to be seen here by all the beautiful women who are about to descend on the pool without being refreshed."

"Thanks, kid." Vinny looked around, furious that he had

fallen asleep outside.

"Do you want me to have coffee and a masseuse sent up to your room, Mr. Smith?"

"I like the way you think, kid. That's okay. Maybe later. I've got something important to take care of this morning, first." Vinny replied.

"Of course. I bartend at night, but I take care of special requests— if you know what I mean— during the day." Devon winked and was shocked at how smoothly those words flowed from his lips. He had someone offer the same to him when he was at the Biltmore with his parents and he repeated the schtick verbatim. Devon couldn't help but wonder why he had even offered. What possessed him to make such an offer? Was it the old adage about keeping friends close and enemies closer? Devon wasn't sure Pinky Ring was either to him, but he knew this man was an enemy of Bria's. An enemy who would soon be looking for the gun that Devon had stolen from him.

His goal was to figure out what was going on and protect the Blooming Sands, yet he hadn't involved security. He hadn't called the police. Instead, Devon stepped deeper into the fray. In the past twenty-four hours Devon had done things he never imagined— and the rush of it all was sending shockwaves through his body. Bria Brigante and the lifestyle he had imagined her living were oddly seducing him.

Mr. Smith seemed as pleased with his offer as Devon was.

"Tell the front desk you want to talk to Devon. I'll find you immediately." Devon continued, shocked with how well he was playing the part.

"Sure, kid." Vinny winked.

Devon walked away worried. What did he mean? What was the important business— with a gun— that Mr. Smith needed to tend to? Devon couldn't help but wonder where he hid the little gun while he laid, passed out on the chaise. Then the terrifying thought of Mr. Smith finding out Paolo handed Devon the much larger gun struck Devon. That's not an order you forget about picking up.

    Devon needed to find Bria and figure out what was next, quickly, before they were both dead. Did she know this man? Was Bria Brigante here on business? Could the scene at the beach the other night have been a setup? A thousand thoughts flooded his brain. If her father was Papà Brigante, then one Blooming Sands location would be chump change for her. There had to be something bigger at stake. The question was, does he show his cards, or does he let Bria play hers?

ROUGH SURF

Bria struggled to hold on. The pressure of the waves relented momentarily, allowing her to push as hard as she could from the sand beneath her. She emerged from the water like a dolphin, gasping for oxygen as fully and completely as she could when she broke the surface. It was then that the other wave landed, throwing her back under. Bria grabbed the jutting formation scarring her back. It was thin and tall. The stone came from the sea like a stalagmite. Bria struggled to get her arms around it. "This is my fate," she thought.

Then she screamed, "PAPAAAAAA!" Her arms captured the formation as her fragile skin broke under its severity.

"PAPAAAAA!" It was then, Bria heard it.

The Ridgeway Hawk soared above her. She had learned that this endangered species was indigenous only to the Dominican. As she clung to her stalagmite, the majestic creature circled above her.

"Caw!" it cried. Its cry calmed her. Her fear was gone. She would either die with her family or live to avenge them.

Bria grabbed the formation hard. The waves seemed impenetrable. She had one hundred feet left until the sand. She could do this. She looked for the shelf. It would be going backward, but she would not go backwards. Bria looked ahead. She needed a strategy. "Caw! Caw!" They were long, thoughtful, purposeful drawls from the creature above. She looked up at the majestic bird watching her. "Yes, Papà. I hear you, Papà."

ANTONIO

"This woman runs like an angry gazelle," Antonio thought as he followed her from a distance. He knew Bria had plenty to be angry about, but he wasn't sure how much she even knew. Antonio could barely keep up. She was fast. He noticed her approaching the cliff and knew it was time for him to stop. She would be turning around, he thought. But she didn't. As Antonio caught his breath in the shade of the palms, he watched Bria Brigante step into the water and brave the fierce surf.

"Lei è pazza!"

Antonio couldn't believe his eyes. This woman was fearless. He chased after her but by the time he got to the bluff, Bria had been washed under by the surf. How would he get to her? He knew he could not challenge the God of the sea. He must get to the other side and see if he could reach her from that direction. Antonio saw a path up the side of the bluff and ran as fast as her could. His legs burned as he sprinted up the steep path. He chased the edge of the bluff, looking for any sign of her. He finally saw her— she was still alive! She had thirty meters to go and she was clinging to a rock. Antonio yelled down to her but the roar of the surf deadened his sound. As he looked around, he found a matching path on the far end of the bluff. He sprinted across the half-built development and raced to the small path. As he started down the hill, his eyes reached for any clue that she was still alive. His lack of attention to his steps allowed a small rockslide to take his feet from under him. Antonio landed on his back, his head crashing against the hard earth. As he tried to get up, his head refused. He used his hands to find something to grab and hoisted his throbbing head upright. His vision became distorted and he fell back to the ground.

STRENGTH

Bria held the rock tightly and looked under water for the next large formation. The next was twenty feet closer to her destination. Bria caught her breath and when the water surges again, she'd push off against the tide and reach for the security of the stone. Eighty feet to go. She tried to repeat her last move, but the next rock was at least forty feet away. She had barely made the twenty. She would have to let the waves pummel her into the crag and strategically push herself from the jagged wall at an angle that would allow the deadly surf to suck her in the direction of the next rock. The rock she clung to was lower and harder to hold onto. She was wasting too much of the energy she had left thinking. She needed to take the leap. As the next wave approached, Bria leapt with all the anger she held inside. She pushed ferociously toward the rock wall. She kicked off the wall with vehemence, toward the next rock. The wave spun her furiously beneath its weight as Bria fought to find the next target. Her shoulder landed the formation as the water receded. Bria fought to grab it but between the pain and the force of the water's pull, she struggled to grab on. As the rock slipped away, Bria caught a smaller stone with her foot, allowing her to push back toward the stone. As she clung in exhaustion to her new pier, she looked for the next opportunity. The beach was within her grasp. Maybe another forty feet? Missing her landing could bring her farther out to sea. She looked for someone, anyone to call to for help. The deserted beach that she longed to reach, the motivation for her current situation, gleamed with untouched sands.

Bria was alone. Again.

The word and the moment seemed a common ailment for Bria—even when she stood amongst crowds, entertaining tourists on the beach. She could depend only on herself.

Bria looked up to the sky at the circling hawk, and with Brigante determination leapt toward the crag, and moved her arms quickly against the formation to pull herself as close to the beach before it would recede again. As her body slammed against the stone and the white surf circled above her head, Bria's fingers lodged in a crevasse and she held with power she didn't know she had until the wave freed her from its bind. She moved quickly against the wall, hoping the next impact would bring her to the safety of the beach. The next wave pushed her forward and her body was rolled free from the crag and slammed on the beach. She had made it. She laid on the beach, allowing the next wave to roll gently over her as she mustered the energy to move. Her body felt as though it had been rolled through a pasta maker. She looked up to the sky and the bird was gone. She found herself on the most incredible beach. Oddly, she knew finally that she wasn't alone. Inside of her was everything she needed.

As she sat, catching her breath on the beach, her father's words came to her,

'*Chi ha fatto il mala, faccia la penitenza."*

Why, when she needed to be focusing on cleaning up her mess, was her father so close to her? '*Chi ha fatto il male, faccia la penitenza."* It meant, when someone has done evil, they must do penance. Bria couldn't help but ask herself where this emotion coming from, and why it was coming at this moment.

DESERTED BEACHES

Bria looked around at her sliver of beach. It may have only been fifty meters, but it was protected by palm trees and overgrown bushes and foliage. It was amazing. She could see no one in either direction. She was sure it seemed as though the beach had stopped sooner, before the crag, because of the overgrown plants. At one end of the beach was the giant cliff, the other was harbored by a combination of hibiscus and palms. Coconuts laid abandoned on the ground, many with new sprouts exploding from the top of their shell, holding a future palm tree trying to rise.

The only footprints Bria saw were her own. There was some freedom in being all alone. Bria took off her running bra and t-shirt. She laid them over a leaning palm to dry. Next, it was her shorts and underpants. Bria stretched her arms above her head and let the warm sea breeze caress her damp skin. Being naked in plain site was glorious. It was empowering. It was freeing. Bria sat on the beach, feeling the sand beneath her buttocks. It was warm, and slightly uncomfortable. She pulled her long hair into a soft pillow to place beneath her head. The morning sun was warm on her body. Her breasts were pale and Bria relished the idea of letting the sun warm her entire body. She had hours before her shift. Bria closed her eyes and let her body melt into the sugar fine sand.

"I see you are trying to attract more sharks. But I wonder, do you prefer land sharks to sea?" Antonio stood beside her. "You are more beautiful in the daylight, Bella."

Bria jumped at his voice and moved her arms forward to

protect herself.

"I noticed it wasn't your chastity you were protecting, Bella."

Bria moved her hands to her breasts and laughed. "I'll take that swim now."

Antonio's clothes came off faster than the night they met. He trounced carelessly in the water and beckoned Bria to follow.

"Come, Bella, come!" Bria was glad for Antonio. Her body quivered at the thought of going back into the sea that almost swallowed her. It was nice to be with someone. Antonio held out his hand as she approached. She was safe with Antonio. This crazy man with a silk scarf and long, flowing brown hair made her feel as though she was home. As she reached out to him, his hand felt like the warm embrace of a friend. She expected him to grab her, pull her near, make passionate love to her while the waves crashed against their exquisite bodies. But he didn't. He grabbed her hand and led her to the deeper water. Bria could feel the anxiety between her legs. Antonio was not responding. He pulled her gently through the waves and released her hand as she floated in the crystal blue waters of the Caribbean. Bria was shocked. She looked Antonio over. Was he interested? Did his body say something that his actions were not? No, Bria thought, they were friends. Why had he had a change of interest, she wondered. It was almost infuriating, but also lovely. Bria and Antonio swam naked in the clear water for what seemed like an hour.

"Why are you here, Antonio? Were you following me?"

"I might ask you the same thing, Bella."

"I almost killed myself getting here," Bria said as she pointed to the treacherous bluffs.

"You are a mountain climber, Bella?" he laughed.

"No, I came by sea, Antonio," she said as she looked toward the crashing waves.

Antonio gasped and then laughed uproariously. "You are lucky you are alive, Bella. I knew you were pazza, but I didn't know how many."

"Much." Bria corrected.

"Yes, you are molta pazza, bella, molta pazza." They both laughed. "I will show you the simple path back," Antonio said.

At that, Antonio's hand accidentally grazed Bria's thigh. Antonio said nothing. Bria waited, but said nothing either. They continued to swim, the graze unmentioned. It was amazing to be so free with Antonio. He didn't care who she was or where she came from, he was only focused on the moment. Bria wondered what his life would have been had he stayed and worked in his family business. As she thought about her family business, she instantly remembered the man sleeping by the pool. She had seen that man before.

BELLA BRIA

The path back to Blooming Sands was a welcome relief compared to what she had experienced earlier. Antonio grabbed her hand and elbow gently as they climbed the hill. He was protective, she liked that. At the top, the homes she had admired sat majestically. The view was as extraordinary as she had imagined. Only half of the homes were built, leaving the most pristine and scenic property undeveloped. Antonio explained this was the government's doing. Permits and conservationists had stalled the project and it was caught up in bureaucratic red tape over concern for the Ridgeway hawk's sanctuary. Bria didn't want to move from that spot. She understood why the hawks loved it so much. From the top of the cliff, she could see for miles in each direction and looking behind her, the landscape was equally spectacular. Miles of green hills carefully descended to sea level. Bria felt as if she could see across the entire island of Hispaniola.

"We stay here all day, Bella? Maybe I'll set up camping?"

"I'm coming, Antonio. Isn't this beautiful?" Bria was breathless.

"Like you, Bella." Bria looked back at Antonio as he said his words. She couldn't figure him out. Was he playing hard to get?

Thinking of the man back at the hotel, Bria suggested she buy Antonio lunch at the Blooming Sands. "How can you say no to a free meal? Especially on your budget." Bria giggled in spite of herself.

They walked back to the hotel. Ahead, of them, Bria watched the beach vendors harassing vacationers. Sometimes there'd be three or four per tourist. As she would step closer, the vendors would scatter. "Still afraid, still annoying others, *Chi di gallina nasce, convien che razzoli*," Bria mentioned aloud.

"I'm sorry, Bella? I don't understand." Antonio asked.

"Oh no, I'm sorry. I was just talking to myself," Bria answered.

"What children are like their elders, bella? The sand fleas?"

Bria giggled. "No, I'm working on a project with the beach vendors. I want to help them but I'm unsure of how to get them to accept my help. If my father was here, he would know what to do. I was just hoping I had a little bit of him in my head right now."

Antonio couldn't hide his interest, "Oh, what kind of project?"

"I'll tell you in a few days."

At that, Antonio gave a knowing smile, as if he knew her better than she knew herself.

As they walked onto the Blooming Sands property, Devon stopped Bria as though he had been waiting for her.

"Is something wrong, Devon?' asked Bria.

Devon had come up with twenty different things to say but none of them was right. And the addition of her newest victim made the conversation even more uncomfortable. Was this man a wealthy tourist? An associate of her father's? It seemed to draw vehemence from within him, that of which he had never experienced before. This woman is trouble. The warning signs kept mingling with another emotion that always seemed to take precedence when he looked at Bria Brigante. There was something about her that never left his brain, and obvious other parts. He kept thinking of Max, and what Max would want him to do. Protect the reputation of the hotel but keep her there driving revenue. Shit.

"No, Bria, enjoy your lunch with your friend. We'll catch up later."

She walked away with her handsome stranger.

GETTING CLOSER

Vinny could smell her perfume. Finally, all of his waiting would finally be rewarded. By now Vinny knew her perfume, her footsteps, and her laugh. This was the daughter of Papà Brigante. He had been loyal to Papà at one time, but Papà turned on him. Now he would finish the job that was started nine years ago.

Bria walked from around the massive blue urn with her wild mane of brown waves just settling from the sea's breeze. She was laughing, he could hear that. Was she working already? Vinny stood from his lounge chair ready to follow her to her room. He put his hand on his tiny gun and checked his other leg for the fishing knife he had bought earlier from one of the natives.

He saw her legs round the urn first. Those long lean legs were her mother's. Finally, she emerged. Vinny couldn't believe what he saw. Bria was not alone, and he knew the man escorting her.

Vinny ducked behind the potted fern just out of sight.

"Why was she with him?" Vinny couldn't get the thought from his head. He watched as the two laughed and talked. They were comfortable with each other. This made no sense. As he watched them sit for lunch, Vinny went to his room to call his boss. This could be a problem.

UNDERCOVER DEVON

Devon watched Bria pull her hair to one shoulder. It was like watching a lion tamer control her beast. He knew every move she had. He was watching her laugh with envy. This time, it wasn't fake. She had two laughs, one when she was being polite and one when she was laughing at her own joke. It was rare someone could make her laugh as hard as she could herself. Her newest victim seemed to be managing fine.

Devon had noticed the man with the pinky ring was back at the pool later that morning. He had sat there for hours focused on two places: the hotel exit and the beach entrance. Devon knew just for whom he was looking, but she was nowhere to be found. The man's clothes were nicely starched and, Devon noticed, were baggy enough to hide the gun that belonged in the case he stored in his room. As Bria and the long-haired model passed the man with the pinky ring, Devon kicked himself for not talking to her when he had stopped her. Thankfully, the presence of a man with her startled Pinky Ring as much as it had Devon. Devon watched as the stocky stalker edged behind the urn, their shapes oddly similar. Devon knew he couldn't let her leave alone. He was about to make his move on Bria— whatever that was supposed to be— until she surprised him with company.

Devon watched "Mr. Smith" walk carefully out of Bria's sight and head to the elevators. Devon couldn't let him out of his sight. As the man stepped into the elevator, Devon stepped into the stairwell and ran to the security office a floor below. His hand banged on the door of the security office with incredible authority. When the first officer opened the door, Devon noticed he had his gun drawn. Devon's pounding must have been a little too aggressive.

"Elevators! The cameras, I need to see the cameras!" Devon didn't know why he was out of breath. It was one floor down and a short run but Devon's heart was racing and his face was hot with perspiration. "There! There! There! What floor is that?"

"Twelve."

"Thank God. Confirm that he goes to twelve-nineteen, OK?" Devon huffed.

"Yes, sir. Room twelve-nineteen. There he goes, sir."

"Thank God. Thank you." Devon's breathing returned to normal momentarily. He then said, "Ping me when he leaves his room." The security guard started to question why they should do that, and Devon merely held up his hand.

"I'm authorized by Max Bloomfield the third. You can confirm this with him."

"Yes, sir," the guard obliged.

Bria and Antonio talked about Italy, corettas, making the perfect espresso, and their parent's love affair with art, classical music and out of place lace doilies. Bria felt like she had a friend who understood her world – as much as anyone could. It was hard to say goodbye to Antonio. She had missed Julia so much. This was the first time she felt any sense of camaraderie since. Julia still avoided her calls and emails, but Bria was committed to winning her back. She needed Julia. They were family, and family meant everything.

She rose from her chair to kiss Antonio goodbye. He graced each cheek with his lips.

"Ciao, Bella."

"Ciao," she whispered, still wondering about Antonio's intention. Something didn't make sense, especially the twenty-dollar tip he threw on the table after their free lunch.

Bria watched him walk away, past the pool, and then the beach bar. Something was wrong. Her intuition told her she was safe with Antonio but things weren't what they seemed. She thought about her overwhelming desire to avenge her family's death and wondered what Antonio would have said if she shared this. She stood gazing toward the beach, trying to make sense of her new friend and her intuition when Devon tapped her on the shoulder, "Come with me."

GUNS

"Why would I go with you?" Bria demanded.

"Please, I'll explain in a minute. Just come." Devon was pleading.

"Coming isn't that easy, it takes two and a very talented man," Bria smiled.

Devon's face didn't budge, "Bria."

"Fine. What is going on, Devon? I know you don't care for me, although you do always seem to be watching. I know you like my legs and you drink Macallan twenty-five."

Devon's face froze. He tried to recall drinking in front of Bria, it was only in the airport. "You remember me from the airport?"

"My father taught me to be observant and trust no one," bolded Bria.

"Well, that might be a useful skill right now." Devon couldn't hold back.

Bria was quiet. The man with the Ferragamo driving shoes came to mind. Now she remembered him from the airport bar as well. The man she saw passed out at the pool. She thought she had seen him on the beach as well, but he didn't seem to notice her. Bria looked around for a way to prepare herself for what was next.

"Where are we going?" Bria demanded. She was wrong, and she was never wrong about men. She had thought Devon was a rich trust fund kid trying to piss off his father.

"Where are we going?" Bria said with more authority.

Devon stopped. "Listen, I know what you can do to men, I've

seen it, remember? I know you could bury me right here in the middle of this hallway, but I need you to trust me. I think you're in trouble. I could be wrong, but I don't think I am."

"The Ferragamo driving shoes? He was behind the potted palm by the pool earlier, wasn't he?"

"Yes, you know him?" Devon said quizzically.

"I think I remember him," she acknowledged.

"He was at the bar at the airport. I heard him make a phone call and then he showed up here. He said you look like your mother." Bria bowed her head slightly and quickly composed herself.

"Who was he talking to?"

"I don't know, but it sounded like his boss." Devon complied.

"Where are we going?" Bria asked again.

"I thought we'd be safer in my room; my guess is he knows your room number. Last I checked, he went back to his room on the twelfth floor after he saw you walk in with your friend. I haven't seen him since."

Bria nodded.

Bria followed Devon to his suite, "Quite the upgrade from the staff's quarters," Bria taunted.

"Why are you so calm?" Devon said in a nervous scream.

"I don't know. Really." Bria paused. "I don't know. I just am."

Bria entered Devon's room. Devon closed the door and locked it behind him.

"Lucky I trust you," Bria smirked. Devon looked at her, bewildered. Bria Brigante had a fierceness to her that he had never seen. He had plenty of women alone in his room before, but this is the first time he was more afraid of the woman in front of him than the gun-wielding stalker looking for her.

"I, uh, got this from a guy downtown. I think he's going to know it's missing soon." Devon went to the back corner of his closet and pulled out a shopping bag.

"You bought me a dress?" Bria joked, again, unnerving

Devon.

He didn't say a word as he handed her the heavy bag. Bria pulled the brown bag out of the shopping bag carefully. It was wrapped in a brand-new beach towel– presumably for the maid's sake. She looked up at Devon without opening the bag and smiled, "Merda! I had you wrong."

"What is that supposed to mean?"

"I had you pegged for a trust fund kid trying to piss off his father, not... well... not this." At that, Devon's eyes darted away. "What were you doing bartending, anyway?" she pressed. Devon knew she had every right. Suddenly, he was not Devon Lancaster. He was not Dylan Lancaster's son: confident Wharton grad, ready to take on the world, and making his own way without the help of his father. Bria Brigante had a way of making him feel like a spoiled trust fund kid acting out and in over his head. Right now, he was exactly who she had thought he was. He needed to step up and show her she was wrong.

"Don't worry about why I'm bartending. There are more pressing challenges right now. Who is this man following you and why is he following you?" Devon puffed his chest up and reclaimed his confidence.

"Well, aren't you full of surprises, Devon Lancaster. Are you going to tell me the truth or shall I spend a little time on Google learning it on my own?" Bria could not be played. She took the gun from the bag and put it in the band of her running shorts. She then grabbed a summer sweater out of Devon's closet and wrapped it around her waist to secure the heavy piece.

"What are you doing with that?" Devon was shocked by her ease.

"Nessuno ti proteggerà tranne te," Bria stated as if he should know it. "My father would tell me, you can only rely on yourself for protection."

It was then Devon knew her father had been Benedetto Brigante.

Bria stared at Devon carefully. She wondered if she could

use him. He obviously was out of his league – and perhaps so was she— but how could she not trust him after he readily handed her a thirty-eight? He could be her eyes. She looked at his lean, tan body and wondered if he could fight. No, the only person he had ever fought was his father. She was sure he had money. That could solve many problems.

"Do you want me to help you get out of here?" Devon asked.

"A Brigante never runs." She paused. "Now tell me your truth, Devon Lancaster. All of it."

VINNY

He watched her leave with the bartender. He wondered if her mother had enjoyed the company of men as much— before she met Benedetto Brigante. He followed the two and watched the elevator move to a restricted floor at the top of the hotel. Why would she be working the beach but have access to a restricted floor? Something didn't make sense. She was following the bartender; was it his room? Why would a bartender have a suite so nice? Was the bartender involved? Vinny recalled the bartender helping him at the swim-up bar and giving him inaccurate information. He would take care of him next. First, he needed to get Bria. If she was staying in the penthouse, she definitely had her father's fortune. But that fortune didn't belong to her – it didn't belong to her father either. It was time for Vinny to give it back to its rightful owner.

Vinny would have to get access to that floor, but to leave the eighteenth floor might mean losing her again. He decided to wait two floors below and watch when the elevator ascended to the top floor. He would then hit the down button, ensuring its passengers were delivered directly to Vinny. There would be more casualties than Vinny liked, but now knowing the other family was here was a problem. It was now or never. Vinny entered the elevator and went to the eighteenth floor. He pitied the maid who passed him next. He wasn't sure what it would take to get the keys from her, but he knew whatever it was, it was not going to be pleasant. His only other option was to intercept Brianna as she attempted to pass him. What he wouldn't do was let her slip by him again.

NEXT STEPS

Bria sat patiently as Devon told her what he knew. It took a while, but she finally identified how Devon would be useful. It helped her see more clearly what Papà would do.

"Pinky Ring probably followed us here." She thought aloud.

Devon was amused by how quickly Bria adopted the name he had given the stocky stalker. It was becoming increasingly evident that he was a hitman. He wanted to ask why he would want to kill her but knew she'd never answer.

"Do you know him?" Devon asked.

"I remember him visiting my father before my father died." Devon was struck by her use of the word father versus family. Bria continued. "He was one of the nervous ones. I remember sitting on the stairs while Papà made him wait. I thought this would be a bad meeting, but to my surprise, I was invited into the office to pour wine." Devon thought of stopping her and asking questions but decided against it. "I can't remember what he said but I do remember Papà saying,

'Mr. Vegas wants to work for me, Bria. Do you think we should let him?'"

Bria was suddenly lost in the moment eleven years ago. She was being a difficult teenager. She remembered shaking her head and whispering to her father that she didn't like him because "he sweats too much." It was then, Bria realized why her father had always invited her in. Her intuition about people, even at a young age, was her greatest gift. Papà knew that, and he used it. Rage took over her emotions. Vengeance filled her face. *Ricorda il mio cognome. Sono un Brigante.*

Devon could feel the change in Bria. She was lost in her head, but her face changed. She was no longer the seductress; no longer a barracuda. What she had transformed into was far more dangerous.

Bria knew Vinny Vegas would be nearby. She told Devon to have a new room arranged for himself on a new floor and move to it as soon as possible. She stormed out the door. She walked to the elevator, focused. Where— was— he?

She didn't know herself right now, but she didn't pause long enough to think about who she had become. She would find him. Vinny Vegas. She remembered his name and could smell his sweat.

Bria stepped into the elevator and as the door closed, she pulled her gun from her makeshift holster. Somehow, she knew how to ready it. Had her father taught her that? She stood off to the side so she could see his hands before she saw him. She felt him near. The elevator smelled of leftover perfume from its previous occupants and the silence within its walls was deafening. She felt the carriage slow to stop two floors down. Of course, Devon's floor was restricted; he would be here waiting for her.

SURPRISES

The door slowly opened, and she saw the fat fingers and the bulky gold pinky ring Devon described. She moved her gun in front of her face and braced herself against the wall of the elevator. She saw a knife in his right hand. He saw the thirty-eight and grabbed his tiny pistol. He was stocky, but strong and vicious. He was not a sand flea; he was not afraid of her.

His tone was ominous, "Your father disrespected me."

Bria grabbed the gun tighter, but her fingers froze. It would be her, or it would be him. As the angry man stepped toward the elevator, Bria locked her finger on the trigger. Bria couldn't speak. The weight of the gun and of what she was about to do were overcoming her. Could she kill a man? Did it matter that it was self-defense? She tightened her grip as Vinny stepped closer to her.

He didn't seem to care that she held a gun. Did he know she had never aimed it at anyone? Was her face giving away her fear?

"I remember you, Vinny." She tightened her grip, "I told Papà not to trust you."

"Your father always thought too much of your opinion, Brianna."

"As it appears, it seems I was right."

"It didn't have to be that way. Your father betrayed me."

"That's not how it looks right now. Who do you work for?" Bria asked. Her anger filled her body and she knew now that she could pull the trigger. Vinny noticed the shift in her posture and stayed silent, as if he was reassessing the situation.

She spoke again, firm and fierce in her tone, "Who do you

work for?" Her voice echoed and surprised her assailant.

"You are just like your father, Bria Brigante."

"Chi di gatta nasce, sorci piglia." The words she hadn't heard in nine years, came easily to her lips. It was then she realized he needed something from her. He wasn't going to kill her— yet. Bria continued, "Why are you here, dishonoring my father yet again?"

Vinny stared at Bria, the first flinch of fear crossing his gaze.

"Where is it, Bria?"

As he stepped closer to Bria with his extended gun, Bria caught her breath, ready to unload a bullet into her attacker. She wanted to know more. She watched as Vinny tightened his grip on the little gun. As he stepped forward, a tanned arm came from behind him, surprising Bria.

Vinny wasn't expecting this and his reflexes seemed to help what happened next. As he twisted to respond to his attacker, the serrated blade that rested against his neck did its work. The man holding the knife used his free arm to pull Vinny away from Bria as the weight of his body shifted. The serrated knife slid across her attacker's throat. Vinny's heavy body fell to the ground, jamming the elevator doors open with his limp body and Ferragamo driving shoes. Bria remained in the corner of the elevator, incredulous. She and her hero locked eyes. There was something in his eyes that she hadn't seen before. How had she missed it?

Her hero held his straw hat up to cover the camera and motioned for Bria to step past the dead body. As she stepped from the elevator, her eyes never left the perfectly tanned man. He held the door open and covered the camera until Bria was out of sight. It was only then that he stepped into the elevator himself, kicking the rest of Vinny's body onto the elevator floor.

THE GAME CHANGED

Bria wasn't sure what this all meant. She remembered all the old gangster movies and suddenly knew what it meant to sleep with one eye open. She wondered if she would have shot him. She wondered what he was looking for. Why now? Nine years later? The past nine years rushed through her brain. The nanny, changing her online name, the mysterious deletion of her old social media accounts and having to start all over, homeschooling, her uncle… her family had hidden her in plain sight. But who did this?

She pulled out her father's leather-bound journal and added more quotes. Things that had come out of her mouth in the last twenty-four hours that she could only credit to Papà. Phrases she didn't expect. One note she made steeled her. She re-wrote it on the last page of the journal: *Chi di gatta nasce, sorci piglia.* What is bred in the bone will not go out of the flesh.

She knew at this moment she was her father's daughter. Papà lived inside her and she would avenge his death.

PLANNING AN EMPIRE

Bria spent the day in her room. She took notes, made charts, and planned her next steps. She needed to be on the beach by three and would not be deterred by yesterday's events. She fashioned a gun holster with two garters but found the gun too heavy and bulky to work. She found a clutch that fit the weapon and fashioned a strap from two Hermès scarves. She could carry it for now, but this couldn't be a permanent option.

Bria looked at her notes. She had been up since two a.m. perfecting her strategy. Bria barely needed to be present to keep the beach clean now. The vendors stayed away, and Bria continued to build business at the Blooming Sands by talking to tourists. She filled her wall with sticky notes of what her customers wanted. There was an opportunity waiting to be seized, but she knew she couldn't do it alone.

Bria called Julia. Her call, like all the past calls, were sent to voicemail after the first ring. Bria knew that Julia hadn't blocked her. This was a good sign. This left her hopeful. Maybe one day Julia would pick up. She hoped that Julia missed her as much as she missed Julia. After yesterday, there were so many questions. Vinny Vegas' murder left even more questions. More dangerous questions:

Why?
What was he looking for?
Who could she trust?

Bria shook off her sadness. She missed her family. Was there something in her apartment in New York she hadn't seen? If only she knew someone who could check. Perhaps it had already been checked? Bria picked up the phone and called her property manager. Why hadn't she thought of that before?

"Where have you been, Bria?" he was nervous.

"I'm having passport issues, I'll be home soon."

"Uh, Bria, tell me where you are. I can help you." He was pleading for an answer.

Bria's senses kicked in. They had been there.

He repeated, "Bria, where are you exactly? Give me your address and I'll send you what you need." Here was a man she had only met twice, once when seeing the apartment and once when signing the lease and picking up the key. He was in trouble.

"George, have you seen my apartment lately?" she asked.

"Yes, yes I have." His voice was nervous.

"George, was it messier than I normally keep it?"

He paused. Bria could tell he was wondering if he should answer the question. They were listening. "I'm sorry, George, I'll get it cleaned up as soon as I get home."

She heard relief sweep over him. "When will you be back?"

"Friday, George. I'll be flying in from Italy."

Vinny Vegas knew where she was. His boss knew where she was; Devon heard him checking in with him on the phone. Why would someone else be pushing the property manager so hard to find out where she was? And, if they were still there, that means they didn't find what they were looking for in her apartment.

Bria needed to assemble her new family and she needed to do so quickly.

She took great care in what she wore that night on the beach. She chose her most conservative dress and pulled her hair up in a smart bun. She chose the only pair of flat heeled sandals she had brought to give her the appearance of someone shorter.

Maybe a split second in delayed recognition would save her life. Bria grabbed her loaded handbag and strode confidently to the elevator. It had been the first time she had been in the elevator since the incident. She stood on the side, prepared for each door opening as she descended to the basement level of the hotel. Her handbag was positioned strategically and the top opened. She was prepared to use the gun, today and going forward. Starting that day, it would never rest more than inches from her grasp.

Devon had called last night to check on her. He assured her that everything had been cleaned up and the security team had no idea she was involved. Because of where she had been standing in the elevator, the cameras looked to show an empty carriage. The hotel security was discreet and used a venomous snake as an excuse to keep the floor locked down while they and the police cleared the mess. Even the cleaning crew had no idea. This was the beauty of a tropical island: Tourism comes before the law. This was something no one wants to get out to the media. This would be helpful for her plan.

The elevator door opened to the basement and Bria made her way to security. Even her coworkers didn't recognize her at first. This was good. After some polite conversation, Bria addressed the head of security.

"I've been thinking, I'm not going to be here much longer. I know my presence has made a significant difference in sales for Blooming Sands. I think it's time to start interviewing for my replacement. I would like to find someone who I can train to take over my business for you."

The pitch was effortless, and Bria was given access to the hotel database of security applicants. Bria spent an hour compiling a list of the names and resumes of the toughest, meanest, and scariest applicants she could find. If their resume didn't include jailtime or bouncer or heavyweight boxer it was cast aside. Bria's next step was a trip to the human resources office.

"Can you set these interviews up for me? Two at a time please, starting tomorrow?"

As she effortlessly commanded employees without as much as a question on their behalf, she rummaged through their supply closet and found a series of empty binders, plastic sleeves, and a hotel camera. She held the camera up and said, "I'm going to use this for a week to take pictures and help me remember each interview."

"Good idea," replied the human resource manager, her eyes blank and methodical. Bria couldn't be sure the manager even knew who was asking or what she was saying. After her initial perkiness, Bria realized the young woman was more of a paper pusher than a leader.

Bria recalled her mother describing some of her model friends, "Ah, Bella, she is only a hot air-a balloon. Filled with the air-a and no-thing else. You, you my bella are filled with intelligenza and beauty."

No one in the human resource office questioned her direction or asked any questions. "Of course, Miss Brigante."

Bria bid farewell to the beautiful balloons and continued on her mission.

She went back to her room to grab her stolen iPad. Now, she had almost forgotten about the elevator and the terrorized property manager back home. She was not ignoring fear. Bria was accepting it and it was fueling her.

Devon sat at the bar next to Bria as she reported to her post.

"Didn't expect to see you here," Devon stated.

"I didn't expect to see you on this side of the bar." Her eyebrows bounced slightly as she answered back.

"Are you okay?" Devon asked.

"What do you think? Do I look okay?"

Devon was speechless. She looked different today, but he couldn't place why. He didn't recognize her at first with her hair pulled back so carefully. "You look beautiful."

"Thank you."

"You're not going to make this easy for me, are you?" Devon asked.

"I don't know what you mean."

BACK IN THE DARK

Bria Brigante was hard to figure out. Why was she here? After yesterday, he didn't expect to see her again. A man tried to kill her on an elevator and she sits fearlessly at the beach bar reporting for duty? She was so focused on what's on her iPad that someone could walk right up to her and shoot her in the head. Devon couldn't help but wonder if she was really as all alone on this island as she said she was. Was someone here protecting her? He knew she'd never tell him the truth, although she got the truth from him. It's hard to lie when a staggeringly beautiful woman is standing in front of you with a big gun.

Devon couldn't help but think about the islanders' fear of this woman. It's like they know there's a bigger force behind her. The Blooming Sands has been free of beach vendors since her first day on the job. It doesn't matter if she is there or not, they know it's Bria Brigante's turf. Devon wondered. Did she feel this, too?

As Devon's mind raced, a man walked up behind Bria. She seemed to sense him behind her and she positioned her body with cat like reflexes into a position of authority. How did she know he wasn't a threat?

She stood. "Yes?"

The man was well-dressed with Gucci sandals and linen pants. He was Dominican but spoke nearly perfect English.

"Miss Brigante, I think I have something of yours. It appears one of my men made a grave error in judgement." Bria looked down at the satchel he held. She recognized it.

"Thank you. I'd like to meet this man."

Devon's head was spinning. What was going on?

"I assure you, he had no idea who you are. You can imagine my surprise when I saw your name. Everything is there, Miss Brigante."

"I know you've heard of me. You have my word, I won't hurt him. I would just like to speak to him. Does he work for you directly?"

"No, he's an independent contractor, I think you call it," responded the man.

"Perfect. Bring him to me, here, tomorrow." Bria reached into the man's pocket and grabbed his wallet. She opened it slowly and took his identification and held it to the light. The man said nothing as she performed a visual inspection confirming his identity. She put his ID in her satchel, "I'll hold this until tomorrow. It's a very good picture of you."

"Of course." The man bowed and walked toward the hotel lobby.

Devon couldn't believe what he had just seen. The idea of processing what he had just witnessed was, well, was that of movies. What had he gotten into? This was a little bit more than embezzlement and bad sales, he thought.

Bria looked carefully over at Devon, "You and I will need to talk on Friday. Make yourself available?" Devon knew this was no question. He had watched this woman transform. The words she spoke in front of him, *Ricorda il mio cognome. Sono un Brigante.* They seemed to fuel something in her. Somehow, it excited him. He feared her, yes, but no longer loathed her. The truth was, this incredibly beautiful woman somehow became more desirable.

The next few days were just as strange as the first. Devon watched from afar as Bria spent time in the business center printing, stuffing plastic sleeves and organizing binders. He watched as she took two men at a time on a walk down the beach. She walked as far as the vendor shanties, lingered a bit, always pointed at the vendors, and then turned around. She took their pictures and organized them in one binder. Why did she need so many binders? But it was her last trip of the day that really piqued his interest. She happened to be walking with the biggest, ugliest two men of the day. Devon was sure they were ex-cons, or worse, her associates. Bria walked down to the shanties and lingered longer than usual with the giant men. Finally, Bria separated from the men and walked to shanties alone. The vendors were horrified. He could tell from their body language that they were trying to escape. They had watched her parade up and down the beach all day with different men, pointing out the colorful shacks and discussing them in great detail while they stood in fear each time. Devon was sure they feared for their livelihood, minimally.

This time, Bria was handing the vendors something. She was handing each person a small slip of paper. As she left the shanties, she demanded each passing vendor come her way. Each did, fearfully. It was then she handed them a small slip of paper as well. As she did, she pointed to her two companions. As she approached Blooming Sands, she shook their oversized hands and transferred the remaining slips to the men. He was sure he watched her hand them American dollars as well. The two men departed, happily, in different directions on the beach.

Devon had to know. He followed one of the men down the beach and watched him stand like a guard at the edge of the Blooming Sands property. As he approached, he saw the man hand out a slip of paper to a vendor who approached him.

"Hey, man!" Devon tried to start a conversation.

"You a vendor?" The enormous man gruffed.

"No," Devon replied.

"Then I have no business wit' you." The giant man turned away.

"Can I ask what you're handing out?"

"I say, I have no business wit' you." This time the giant man leaned forward toward Devon.

Devon retreated, "Okay, okay, sorry, man."

Devon walked the beach looking for a vendor with a slip from Bria. A frail woman clasped her paper in one hand with her small daughter in her other.

"Ma'am, excuse me, ma'am?" Devon tried getting her attention.

"No no, I see you wit her, I be dare tomorrow, I swear. I need to feed my children. I be dare."

"Be where?" Devon asked.

"I be dare at the right time wit' my tings. I be dare."

At that, the woman scurried away from him, fearful of not only Bria, but Devon as well.

When Devon walked back to the Blooming Sands, Bria sat under a cabana with the man from yesterday and a bartender he recognized from his bonfire chat. The beach waiter guarded the cabana, but Devon wasn't sure if this was intentional or not. Finally, the bartender left with his head down. He looked up at Devon as he passed.

"I knew I shouldn't trust you, mon. You are no brothah." Devon looked at the cabana and watched Bria in deep conversation with Gucci sandals. As he watched from the bar, he wondered what happened to her Italian playboy. Where had he gone after the day in the elevator?

Gucci sandals stood up and kissed Bria's extended hand, bowing. Her power was undeniable. Bria looked at Devon at the bar and pointed toward Devon, said something quick to her new acquaintance, then sent him off. Bria sat on the chaise under the cabana while her guardian waiter delivered a cool cloth and a fresh glass of Champagne.

Bria did not look back at Devon again.

OUR FATHER

Bria woke with the excitement of a schoolgirl. Who would have known this would be so fun? She laughed as she thought of Devon watching every move she had made throughout the day yesterday. She wondered what he was thinking. After Vinny Vegas, she knew what he was seeing must have looked like a *GoodFellas* movie. She laughed at the thought. He'd learn soon enough, but at that moment, she would enjoy keeping him in the dark. Poor little rich kid, she thought. It was then when she realized what Vinny wanted.

Bria always assumed her father's brother, Salvatore, got all her family's money. When she was seventeen, she didn't care about money, she had just lost her family. When Papà died, Uncle Sal brought her to see an attorney and made her sign what seemed like hundreds of papers. She can still remember the old office with huge leather chairs that swallowed you whole. From the chair where Bria sat, she could see the carousel in Central Park. She sat in the big chair remembering the last time she and Papà had been on the carousel. He had business near the park and insisted she join him. She told him she was too old for the carousel, but he made her ride anyway. As she sat in the attorney's office, she stared out the window, begging for her father to be returned to her. She swore she'd never say no to him again. Her heart wept as Uncle Sal and the old attorney talked and talked at her. A week later, Uncle Sal had a mysterious accident and drove off a bridge. That's when her aunt shipped her off to the nanny in the New York apartment.

Bria's memories poured in. Victoria and her mother didn't

think Bria got Uncle Sal killed. They thought she was holding out on them.

"Tell me the truth, Bria! Tell me the truth!" her aunt ranted when Bria had called to let her know she was safe. She continued, "I know you and that old lawyer are keeping it from me! Where is it?"

Finally, finally Bria understood. It wasn't because she left their home in the middle of the night. They didn't blame her for her uncle's death. Her aunt and Victoria weren't talking to her because they thought she was keeping the Brigante fortune from them. This must be what Vinny wanted. There must be a key or something, somewhere. Bria wondered if she could remember where the old attorney was.

Right now, she had two goals: Build some revenue and don't die.

Her mind raced. Just then, her father's words came to her, *Chi due lepri caccia, l'una non piglia, e l'altra lascia,* you must not run after two hares at the same time. Bria knew what Papà would do.

Bria walked to the beach with a binder and the hotel camera. She entered the cabana that stood furthest to the right on the beach, shielded from the sun by beautiful palms. The extended shade made the breeze cooler in this spot— and to see who occupied it, a little more difficult. The beach waiter, who was now eating filet mignon with his family because of Bria's special skills, set a beautiful tray of fresh fruit and cheeses on a small table in the cabana. He also had an array of Champagne, fresh orange juice, and sparkling water on ice waiting for her. Bria's ability to take care of people evoked unwavering loyalty. She made promises, and she kept them.

This was Bria's moment of truth.

A small, slightly overweight woman of forty was her first meeting. She came in with her two daughters.

"Hello, what is your name?"

"Miranda."

"Hola, Miranda. Who are these little angels you have brought here?"

"Oh, I am so sorry missus, I have no camera for taking photos. I show you on mi hijas. Esta Carmella y Carlotta." Her nervousness tickled Bria.

"It's OK, Miranda. I want to help you. You see, the hotels hired me to keep you off their beach because it scares customers. But customers, they still want things — like hair braiding and art. That makes their trip special. I want to help you make more money, but also do my job. Do you understand?"

"Yes, missus, I tink so. But how will you make more money for us?"

"You'll have to trust me. But for me to help you make more money, I need to earn money as well."

"I understand."

Bria took out her first sheet of paper and put the number one in the first box she had set aside for a photo. It was labeled "Vendor." Above the box, Bria wrote "Miranda." She then took pictures of the children's braids and labeled the next two boxes two and three. Above these boxes were the words "Product." Bria continued to ask a series of quick questions and within ten minutes she was done.

"Miranda, I know you are scared and this is a big risk. I want you to ask Ricardo, the waiter outside here, about my word. My word is my blood. Without my word, I have no life."

"Tank you Miss Bria, tank you. I believe in your word Miss Bria." Bria held Miranda's hand lovingly and told her everything would be okay, and Miranda left.

The next vendor would be more of a challenge and in some cases she'd need to call in Ricardo to translate. By the end of the day, Bria was exhausted. She had met with vendors every ten minutes since early that morning and had signed over sixty vendors. The next day would be more of the same. The next day, vendors from Santo Domingo sought out Bria and asked for similar assurances.

After two days, Bria had met with two vendors at a time, no longer needing to explain, and had signed one hundred and twenty-two beach vendors and eighteen drug dealers. Bria was now in the larimar, greenstone sculptures, handmade jewelry, hair-braiding, basket weaving, mamajuana, painting and marijuana business. She could arrange boat tours, scuba-diving, clamming, and booze cruises. If you wanted to go deep sea fishing or get married, Bria Brigante now owned a piece of that business as well. No tourist in the Dominican could do anything unless Bria got paid.

She would reward Ricardo as soon as she could. His help had been invaluable in building the islanders' trust, just as it kept the sand fleas from revisiting the Blooming Sands. She imagined what he must have said to the islanders. She was regularly surprised by his ability to get their attention. She had asked him once.

"Ricardo, what is it that you say to these vendors, so they don't come to our beach?"

"Oh, Señorita Bria, I just tell dem' da trute."

"Well, what truth is that, Ricardo?"

"Oh nothing, señorita. I just make them real sure that they know not to mess wit' you. Señorita Bria, you are my family." At that, Ricardo bowed while smiling slyly. Ricardo would be the first one she paid.

That coming Monday, Bria would send her two new security recruits to collect. Bria took a risk that their collections would cover what she promised to pay them. She told the vendors that she would send collectors every Monday. If she found out they were being dishonest and holding back money, she would end their ability to do business in the Dominican and Haiti. She also told them she or one of her men would come and visit them. Not doing business was one worry for the islanders, but their fear of Bria was far greater. By Monday, Bria planned to reward them with new opportunities to sell more of their product and live up to her word.

After two days of meeting with her new associates, Bria got to work. She sorted her binders by quality of product and kept a special event tab at the back of each of them. She created beautiful, Madison Avenue quality product sheets for each vendor and organized them strategically. She needed Friday to go seamlessly, and by this weekend, she would be meeting with hotels.

Bria had done her homework. She knew what the tourists wanted and what the hotel owners needed. She had an army of vendors, who, when directed and organized, could cater to any demographic. She would teach them how to negotiate and eliminate the desperation with which they lost their power with the tourists and cost themselves profit. Bria also knew that Max Bloomfield II was coming in Friday afternoon to golf with one Devon Lancaster. Bria assumed he was going to make a play to hire Devon– which would certainly piss off Dylan Lancaster– unless Bria could convince Devon that there was a better way to infuriate Daddy.

Devon sat in the outdoor veranda waiting for Bria. He ordered an orange juice and tried to focus on the warm breeze versus his week of spying, guns, and murder. Devon was sure to take a seat closest to the stone wall where he would safely keep his back. He grabbed his hands, so they'd stop trembling and tried to remember that he was a Wharton grad– just like her. He was smart– just like her. He was confident– just like her. He mentally banged his head as he tried to convince himself that he was better, stronger, smarter and richer. But one thing he knew as the truth was that he was not like her. He wasn't quite sure if anyone could be.

He kept trying to forget the ease with which she handled the killing machine. He watched her chew up a criminal and vow allegiance from two other criminals. He watched the old man with five kids who waited on tourists at the beach, stand over her like a father and believe in her like a god.

Bria Brigante was under everyone's skin; she was like a drug. One knew they should look away and stay away, but her presence pulled you in. You could feel the intoxication before you're close enough to taste it. And now? She was asking for a meeting with Devon.

What was she up to?

"I never thanked you." Bria said as she walked up to Devon's table.

"No need, I welcome the adventure." Devon returned. Bria had a smart tennis outfit on. He was surprised she owned one, but nothing could truly surprise him about Bria Brigante any longer. The question was, was she there to do harm to Blooming Sands or did she have other business?

Bria knew the way to influence men, but Devon was different. She knew she couldn't impress him. She knew not to feed his ego and she knew she couldn't bullshit him. That's why she liked him most. She needed to be the one person he trusted. It wasn't that he wasn't trusting, he just didn't trust anyone's motives. He was extremely cautious. He was also as greedy as his father. She would have to play him differently. Devon Lancaster had women chasing him. His social accounts were never posts by him, but of him. He was tagged by women of all races, ages, and standings. His world was prim and proper. There was never a post of him partying or having too good of a time. He was of good lineage and cautious in the public lens. But one thing was clear. He wanted more, and he wanted people to know he was worthy of it.

"Well, this is an adventure not many people can handle," Bria responded finally.

"Did you find out what that man wanted? And who was the other guy?"

"I might have an idea about his motive, but I still don't know who the man is who saved me." She was careful not to say "kill."

"What is your idea?" Devon leaned forward. Bria decided to confide in him while selling her skills and before answering his question:

"My father was a powerful businessman. He was killed nine years ago, along with my mother and sister." Bria paused, catching her breath as her eyes filled with tears. She continued, further disarming her target. "I should have been in the car with them that night. I didn't know all the details until years later when I read about it. I thought it was an accident and, I guess, I was protected from the truth. I was sent to the city to live with my nanny and be homeschooled. After I graduated and started working, my family's careful plan to hide me in plain sight was foiled as I started receiving awards for my marketing campaigns for major global accounts. Anyway, I believe that's how they found out I was still alive. Whomever sent Pinky Ring believes I still hold onto something that they want."

Devon sat stunned. "Did you know you were being followed?"

"I saw Pinky Ring outside my apartment the night before I left to come here. But no, I didn't connect it all until I saw him duck behind the palms. I still didn't know who he was until you and I started talking, and then the memories flooded in." Bria was careful to only share what he would have deduced from an internet search.

"Now what?" Devon asked, hoping the story wouldn't end there.

"Now I build a business here."

Devon was shocked and his voice quickened, "I don't understand? You're not safe here. That man worked for someone. That someone knows where you are."

"That someone killed my family. I won't be safe anywhere."

Silence followed. Devon sipped his orange juice.

"I'm sorry," he said finally. "But maybe you should move hotels at least? Eliminate some risk?"

"I can't, Devon. It's complicated. I promise to share the story over a glass of wine one day when we have more time. Trust me, Devon. I cannot."

"So how can I help?" Bria knew this question was a good sign. She had to be careful how she phrased it, or Devon would know her motives behind her sharing were tainted.

"Well, I've been working on an idea that I think will be a huge benefit to all resort hotels with more discerning guests. I've organized my plan, have got everyone in place, and now just need a broker to help flip the switches. Maybe you could connect me with someone?"

"I've been meaning to ask you what you were doing. Something with the vendors, I assume?"

"I'm surprised you haven't asked. You're not a very discreet spy." She smiled.

"I wish I had taken that class on espionage at Wharton." They both laughed.

"Why didn't you just ask me, Devon?"

"Truthfully, I wasn't sure I really wanted to know."

Bria opened her tennis bag and pulled out three binders. She also pulled out several marketing mockups she created with the limited resources of the Blooming Sands Business Center. "It's not as nefarious as you think."

"Wow. You did this all in the last few days?" Devon looked at the tidy binders with vendor details he had never expected.

"Devon, how much money do you think I will earn for the Blooming Sands in a year's time?"

"I don't know, a quarter of a million?"

"Devon, don't play me!" Her hand hit the table, rattling the silver and attracting attention of the patrons around them. "I know you may be pretending to be a bartender, but I know you're better with numbers than that." The irritation rose in her voice. "Your take at the bar and the beach are both up over six thousand dollars each day. Simple math would say I will personally generate close to four million dollars for Blooming Sands. And you know this does not include additional revenue from increased hotel reservations and the overflow of guests to the main restaurant after they leave your bar. Had this not been the case, after our event earlier this week, I would have been kicked off the property. But, I'm special, Devon. This I know. And, I know more people who are like me, and I can create more who can replicate my results. Oddly enough, because of new laws on these ridiculous islands, the hotel cannot manage these problems alone. They need my company."

"Your company?" Devon asked, somewhere between impressed and incensed. The irony that she was doing exactly what he had hoped to accomplish infuriated him.

"Yes. My company. Effective today, I own the beach vendors. I have the power to help, or even hinder, every property on this beach and most of Santo Domingo."

Bria could feel the emotion rising from within Devon's cool exterior. He was trying to mask it, but his business brain was fully activated. She knew she was walking a fine line.

"You have watched me. Hinderance hasn't been my style. This is an amazing business opportunity, but I need help. Quality help. I already have José and Leandro. I will hire protection Monday. I have a few candidates. I also have replacements for myself here at Blooming Sands."

"Replacements?" Devon repeated, emphasizing the plural form.

"Yes, Devon. As I have said, I am special. I have a group of promotional professionals ready to fly here. Of course, now that we understand my value, our rates will change."

Devon laughed, "Of course they will."

Bria could see Devon calculating the profit. He looked up at her skeptically, yet when he looked at the evidence she presented in her binders and promotional tools, he couldn't feign his greed. He wanted a part of what she was creating. He saw his fingers moving, she knew he was counting his contacts.

"Blooming Sands has nineteen properties in the Caribbean alone." His statement was meant to stay in his head.

"I'm aware. I know three others are significantly affected

by this same problem. As my army grows and I take over commerce on each island, I'm sorry to say, it may create a ripple effect for the other properties. I will be able to help them as well, of course." Bria sounded more like her father than she expected.

"I assumed that was your next step. What kind of broker would you be needing?"

Bria had him.

Bria and Devon spent the next two hours lost in strategy. She knew she needed to get him completely up to speed, so he could pitch it to Max II on the golf course later today.

KILLER, OR HERO?

Bria couldn't get her mind off her hero. She hadn't recognized him at first. He wore a beige ball cap and all linen. He blended perfectly into the background, which would make it hard for security cameras in the island resort to isolate specific characteristics. Bria had never known him to dress like this, but it was as if he knew what was going to happen and where it would happen.

Bria couldn't get the image out of her mind. The muscular tan arm reaching around Vinny and the large blade capturing his angular jugular vein. She felt like it happened in slow motion as the serrated blade rippled through his skin and then through his veins. Bria had never imagined so much blood could come from one cut. The elevator door stayed open long enough for her to see it pulse out of him. As it closed, she locked eyes with the killer. But was he a killer? Was he a hero? And just as importantly, why was he there?

Bria had to rely on her instincts if she wanted to be successful. Maybe she distracted the New Yorkers who were looking for her for a few days. Hopefully she threw them off track when she spoke to her property manager. She was careful these days to use a burner phone to make calls and to keep them quick. She wasn't sure what she was dealing with here, or back home. The only thing she did know was that her life was spared. This meant one of two things. There was someone here protecting her, or there was someone here that wanted what they thought she had more than Vinny Vegas and his boss.

She also knew, that time was of the essence and without

money she was powerless. Her jiu jitsu training and a thirty-eight would only protect her for so long. Her attackers were far stronger than her butterfly twist kick and grappling training. She needed a better plan.

She knew the islanders would deliver on Monday. She wasn't sure how she knew, but she did. José and Leandro were all she could afford on her Blooming Sands budget and with the cash that was returned to her from her newest associate. A bodyguard must be her next expense. She had no doubt that by Monday she would have more pressing issues, so this weekend had to be focused on building loyalty. She may need them for more than their goods. *Lealtà e famiglia, Bella, è tutto.*

Bria looked at her watch. Devon would be golfing with Max Bloomfield II now. She had two hours before she needed to be at the clubhouse. She knew what to wear and had enough information from Devon to close the deal. She took her poppy red Cushnie Et Ochs dress from the closet and inspected it before hanging it on the door. She had found a rectangular clutch in the boutique that could double as a portfolio and matched her dress. It was ordinary, but Bria was quick to add a Hermès bow that moved it to extraordinary. She put a mock proposal for one of Blooming Sands' competitors along with an elegant merchant event. The event married elite gifts from the hotel boutiques with high-quality authentic Dominican crafts. It would be an outdoor evening event draped with servers and unique lighting. One glance and even the most discerning guest would put it on their to-do list. Bria knew this life from the time with her family. She knew what it was like to gather baubles on vacation, go to elegant events, and shop at Champagne and caviar riddled art shows. She knew this life and wanted it again. She didn't only want the things that her father's business awarded her family, she wanted them. She wanted her family. She would dream of these elegant affairs and weave them into her marketing strategy. Her vision and eye for elitism helped her create highly publicized events for Italy's most exclusive companies through Vicci. In two hours, she would convince Max Bloomfield II to deliver this to his guests in the Dominican.

Bria moved carefully to her window and surveyed the property. She listened at the door that was locked and chained. She slid the overstuffed chair in front of the door as she had since the attack, adding seconds more to her escape time. Then Bria and her thirty-eight entered the bathroom where water was already filling the oversized tub. As Bria slipped in to the scented water, she closed her eyes and dreamed of her family.

Would Bria Brigante ever feel safe again?

THE CLUBHOUSE

He watched Bria walk into the clubhouse in the dress he had come to know well. He knew this dress meant business. Bria wanted something, and she was about to get it. He watched her enough to be able to predict her behaviors. He had had to do things on this job that he had never expected. Bria Brigante wasn't ordinary. Bria Brigante was just like her father.

He watched Bria enter the room, and he lowered his head as she surveilled the space. He sat with a family he had befriended earlier that week. To them, he was a fellow golf aficionado who always wore boring golf clothes and a straw hat but told great stories. He earned their company and camouflage with his wit and charm, the same way he'd find camouflage with beautiful women, groups of golfers, small children, and employees. He had become the master of deception.

As he watched Bria's eyes pass him, he knew he had succeeded once again. He had to be someone she wouldn't care about. Today, sitting with the Brannigans from Bloomington, Indiana, and wearing a polyester golf shirt, she wouldn't look twice. Yesterday, he was half naked on the beach with a white and black American bandana tied on head and entertaining three young women who were enjoying his pecs.

He knew from her composure she was about to eat another man alive, so today was not the day to interrupt her, to share with her what she needed to know. But still, he could not risk losing her. He needed to find out what she knew. He had been assigned to her since she received an award for her work in advertising. He wondered when they would want him to make his move on her.

Two Brooklyns and a Bottle of Wine

Devon had sat through many courses on sales and persuasion. He studied the psychology and structure of deal-making, negotiating, business law and principle, and a plethora of other courses to help you close deals, make money, and rule the world. But what he had just witnessed could not be taught.

As Max Bloomfield II patted Devon Lancaster on the back for a game well-played and a job well done, Bria Brigante held court at the club bar. He watched her shake someone's hand as though they just sealed a deal. She turned and feigned surprise to see the two gentlemen walking in.

"Mr. Bloomfield, this is Bria Brigante. She was the contractor I had mentioned while we were golfing."

Max Bloomfield II hesitated. He looked at Bria momentarily before reconnecting to his business head. "Miss Brigante, I've heard many great things about you."

Bria looked back at the man she had just shook hands with at the bar, and then back to Max Bloomfield II. "And I of you. I appreciate the opportunity you have given me. I'm honored that I have the opportunity to thank you before I go."

Max Bloomfield looked confused. "Go? But we just got here?"

"No, Mr. Bloomfield. The reason I took the assignment was because I had passport issues, normally my firm would have taken the contract. My issues have been resolved so I'll be sending my replacements to your resort next week. It's an honor to meet you personally, I've understood our work has generated the additional revenue you had hoped."

"Wait, Ms. Brigante..." Max Bloomfield II pleaded.

"Bria. Please." Bria gained more power with her simple response.

"Bria, then. Please join us for a cocktail before you leave? Allow me to thank you properly. Besides, Devon has told me of some other elements of your business that might interest us."

Bria glanced at Devon appreciatively.

"Of course. I'd be honored." Bria bowed her head with power. This power did not go unnoticed to Devon. She was masterful.

Bria ordered a Brooklyn and Devon quickly added, "She prefers hers with Macallan twenty-five."

Max Bloomfield looked at Bria, "Is this true?"

"Yes, but I would never be so presumptuous to order it that way. I already appreciate your generosity, greatly." Devon almost spit out his water. She was an expert.

Max Bloomfield responded obligingly, "If it is Macallan twenty-five you desire, you should have it." As the waiter left, Max Bloomfield couldn't resist learning more about this mysterious business woman.

"Have you ever had Macallan twenty-five straight? Many scotch whiskey makers would believe your order to be a sacrilege."

"My father only drank two things: Macallan twenty-five and wine. Wine, he would say, was only for family. When he taught me about whiskey and scotch, he used to add a cherry to lessen the punch. Now that he's gone, the Brooklyn seems an homage to his memory and seems to make him feel closer, even from the heavens."

Max Bloomfield II was speechless. Devon could not imagine her father being anywhere near heaven right now and now wondered if his daughter would stand a chance either. As her drink arrived, Max Bloomfield II raised his Macallan twenty-five to her Brooklyn and toasted, "To a remarkable man, may he see his impact through your shining light."

Devon couldn't believe what came next. Bria pitched her entire strategy and Max Bloomfield had no other response but yes. Devon wasn't sure if she left him no choice or whether she was casting magic through her olive complexion. Although this was not the first time he had seen that dress on her, it cast the same spell. Devon Lancaster wanted Bria, but was she within his reach?

As Devon sat in amazement— and lust— Bria Brigante and Max Bloomfield II closed a four-hotel deal with more to come. Devon quickly added up his take only to realize that Bria Brigante had matched what he had spent seven years squirreling away in one week. Bria negotiated a percentage of the sales increases and event management contracts that would reap additional sales. He knew she was also getting twenty-five percent of the beach vendors' sales, of which she probably just doubled with Blooming Sands alone.

Bria shook Max Bloomfield's hand, then Devon's. "*Nel successo, nella lealtà e nel sangue.*" It was clear neither Max nor Devon understood her words, but Devon would remember them forever. Bria smiled, "It means in success, in loyalty, and in blood. It was my father's way of welcoming people to our family."

At that, Max Bloomfield II gestured for the waiter, "I want the best bottle of Italian red we have," and then looking at Bria said, "I think it's time we shared a glass of wine."

"Saluti," Bria smiled and tipped her glass again.

One thing Bria had decided to change was how much she drank. It was a conscious decision, but not an easy one. After two Brooklyns and a bottle of Masseto Toscana with her new business partners on Friday, Bria knew she had overdone it. She couldn't protect herself in this state. The men coming for her weren't merely grabbing her ass, they were professionals. They were coming to kill her. The walk back to her room was harrowing and her paranoia was getting the best of her. She felt someone circling, watching. She was thankful for Devon's company as she got to the elevator. She could never make that mistake again. Going forward, things had to be different. This week, whomever searched her apartment in the city would be arriving and she would need to be prepared. She hadn't been careful about her travel plans. When she made the plans, she didn't know she needed to be. So much had changed in the past month, especially Bria. But one thing hadn't changed: She was a Brigante. She would not run.

The meeting with Max Bloomfield II would just be the beginning. The next day, Bria and Devon would meet with each hotel manager to set up events and assign vendor locations on the beach at each hotel. The new partners helped their new clients understand the possibilities that existed if they didn't comply. Bria had a way of explaining this that wasn't part of the Wharton curriculum. Her chillingly calm voice matched her new stance. Her body shifted seriously, something in her eyes deadened, and she explained in a tone that paralyzed her audience, "I would hate to see what might happen if your guests realized that—because of your decision today—there would be no way for them to experience the many island traditions. As of yesterday, I—" Bria pauses and smiles, "I control all of the island traditions." Her steely gaze closed deals.

The way she said it gave Devon chills up his spine each time he heard it. It wasn't a sales pitch. It was a threat. Her confidence was merciless. The response was always the same. First, the manager would look at Devon for his reaction. Devon naturally shrugged his head and bowed. The manager would then look at Bria.

When the managers first encountered Bria, they were mesmerized. Their eyes— regardless of their sex— would cruise from her long dark hair to her breasts to her legs and then back to her eyes. Her eyes would be penetrating them. After she helped them understand the consequence of their actions, and after the quick glance toward Devon, their heads always seemed to move back on their shoulders like a turtle retracting in its shell. The look in their eyes changed from lust and wonder to fear. She didn't verbally threaten them – so to speak – but the aura in the conversation changed. After their pain and their fear was swallowed, the manager would inevitably gather himself and respond,

"This seems like it might be good for our hotel. I'll have my events team get you what you need, right away."

Brigante Enterprises was solving a problem for these resorts. That message coupled with an incredibly handsome frat boy and a fabulous, finessed, yet oddly frightening, marketing exec were no match for the hotel management teams.

By Monday, Bria Brigante would have good news to share with her vendors. She would also make calls to her promotional model agency contact in New York to send talent. Devon would start brokering deals with other hotel chains and manage the legal and government challenges. Bria knew what she had started, and she wasn't close to being done.

DRIVING SALES

Devon and Bria spent the next fifty-five hours together. They barely slept, and to Bria's point, "Who says a manager cannot talk business at ten o'clock on a Sunday night? Nobody, that's who."

Devon was in awe. Bria would close the deal and when the events manager was sent out, Bria would stay five minutes and move to the next hotel. Devon was left planning details while Bria started working on the hotel next door. Bria laid out the plans perfectly, and all Devon would need to do it make sure they had tables ready for the vendors at set times on Monday. By the time Devon made it to the next hotel, Bria was already using her closing line. It was then he'd get the look, Devon would shrug and lower his eyes, and fear would overtake another manager.

The funny thing about Bria was, she wasn't really threatening anyone. She was helping everyone. She just wasn't patient enough to go through the steps to help them better realize what was happening. It took exactly forty-nine minutes to close the sale and set up the next week's events. By Sunday night, the duo had twenty-two hotels ready to go.

Just before midnight Sunday, Bria and Devon sat in her room completing vendor assignment sheets for Monday morning's collection. Each vendor was told to meet José and Leandro on Monday morning at the shanties at eight a.m. It was a deadline no one would miss. José and Leandro would hand out their weekly assignments as they made their first collection. If there were vendor sheets left, they would know who was left to find.

Bria had thought of everything.

As midnight moved to two a.m., Devon and Bria started to get punchy. Bria called for room service and ordered two Brooklyns and a chocolate lava cake.

"I'm sorry, Miss Brigante, the kitchen is closed."

"I'm not sure you understood. I'm Bria Brigante. You might want to rethink your response."

Ten minutes later an older man with orthopedic black shoes showed up smiling at Bria's door. Devon could never be prepared for the way Bria responded to the knock. Devon had no idea she had carried the gun he had given between her legs. Bria lifted her long leg to the bed and grabbed the pistol from the garters that secured it on her upper thigh. Devon's heart raced as she removed it. She held it toward her chest as she peeped through the hole. She smiled, and moved the gun to her back as she let the waiter in.

"Oh, I'm sorry Miss Brigante. The girl at the front desk is new. She didn't know who you are."

"It's okay, darling Jesús. I'm just so happy to see you."

Devon couldn't help but wonder how this dwarfish man with a slight limp knew her so well. He was under her spell.

As he watched, Devon wondered if she was twenty-something or sixty-something. Bria was different from anyone Devon had ever known, and she knew it.

After Jesús left, Bria patted the bed and invited Devon to sit next to her. She handed him a spoon and smiled. "Don't worry, I won't bite."

"You do. I actually think you might do more than bite, Bria."

As Devon called her by her first name, he knew it sounded wrong. They were business partners, he would never call her Miss Brigante. Bria looked up at him, her eyes glistened from the moonlight that sought them out through the window. As she looked his way, Devon was lost in her beauty. The seductress, he thought. Here he was, lying in her bed with her, sharing dessert, sharing a business… could there be more?

Bria moved the "perfect bite" from her spoon to Devon's mouth. Devon couldn't help but close his eyes as he tasted it. He wanted so much more. He was shocked by his lust for her. But then again, she terrified him.

Bria lifted her perfectly made Brooklyn and toasted their successful day. "*Nel successo, nella lealtà e nel sangue.*"

Devon wasn't sure why, but he knew at that moment, he would kill for Bria Brigante.

By Monday afternoon, vendors who feared her now stopped and bowed to her as she passed, and Bria Brigante received her first meaningful paycheck.

QUANDO ANDATE A CACCIA DEVI ESSERE TU A DETTARE LE LEGOLE

When You Hunt; Let the Game Come to You

Bria would wait. They would be here soon. She couldn't understand why they had waited nine years. Why now? What were they looking to find? If her father had hid money, did they think he would have hidden it the mattress or in shoeboxes in Bria's closet? After nine years, Bria couldn't imagine she wouldn't have stumbled across whatever they sought.

Bria lost herself in memories. The week leading up to her family's murder was different from all others – or did it just seem that way nine years later? Papà had known something was going to happen. This was the week he gave her the journal. There were still so many things, so many conversations they had yet to have. There were conversations Papà had wanted to have but Bria, at seventeen, was too busy to hear.

Five days before her family's murder, Bria was in her bedroom with the seamstress, putting the final touches on her prom dress. As she stood in her bedroom, the seamstress her mother had hired to design the perfect dress, was tightening the loose edges with long straight pins when Papà entered the room.

"No, Papà! I want it to be a surprise!"

"Bella, my beautiful Bella. You always surprise me, il mio amore. I just want to talk to you for a moment."

Papà handed Bria a leather-bound journal. The leather was lambskin and its softness inspired Bria to touch it to her cheek. The light tan hide was collected by two strings fashioned from the same skin. The pages were filled with beautiful paper, so beautiful that only a skin so fine could harness its elegance.

"Keep this with you always, Bella, always. It will help you when you need it. Keep in it all the lessons that you have learned, Bella." At seventeen. those words meant nothing. Bria was excited for her prom, she wasn't in the mood for a lecture from Papà. How she regretted this now.

"Papà, did Mama tell you I helped design the dress with Isabella?" Bria looked at Isabella, the seamstress, as she boasted.

"Si, Signore Brigante, this is the creation of your talented daughter. I just helped sew it together." The seamstress smiled coyly and lovingly at Bria.

"Bria. Bella Bria. You are brilliant. Promise me we'll talk after your masterpiece is completed this evening? I have some... I have some business I want to discuss with you, Bella."

"Business, Papà?"

"Yes, you'll understand when I show you. *Chi di gatta nasce, sorci piglia.*" As he finished his sentence, he sent Bria a loving look and walked from the bedroom.

Isabella repeated, "*Chi di gatta nasce, sorci piglia.* What is bred in the bone will not go out of the flesh. Bria, he's right, you are your father's daughter. Sei così bella."

Bria smiled and twirled to see her masterpiece in the full-length mirrors. Bria never went to her father's office that evening. When Isabella left, she immediately called Julia and they talked into the night. Bria told her about the dress, about Jonathan and about whom the limo should pick up first. She did not visit Papà in his office that evening, nor would she the next. Bria would never forget that mistake. What was the business he needed to discuss, Bria wondered? Could that conversation have helped her today?

She wondered who would help her now. She wished Julia would pick up the phone. She had thought, for a moment, that Antonio could fill the hole in her heart that was left by Julia, but for a week, Bria has not seen Antonio. Was he lying in wait as well? She needed to find him, but her instincts told her to wait. Could he somehow be involved? Her brain goaded her to run, but her instincts did the opposite. If Antonio wanted to hurt her, he had had ample opportunity. She had been alone with him several times. They had soul-bearing conversations while they walked the Dominican sand. Perhaps he was simply more patient than the others? Perhaps he was waiting for Bria to reveal where her family's fortune was hidden? Perhaps…

Bria stopped herself. Antonio wasn't a threat right now. The immediate threats were on their way from New York and she needed to be prepared. She knew Papà would be happy to see her putting business before all else. Bria would ensure her business team was in place before she met her new bodyguard the next day. She would make sure Devon had a plan to run the business and the team could collect in her absence. She needed to make sure Devon was protected; she was sure he had no idea how to do this on his own.

She picked up her phone and dialed Julia's number.

"Hello?"

Bria was numb when she heard her voice. She struggled to form words.

"J…Julia. It's me. Don't hang up. Please Julia, if you ever loved me, please don't hang up. I'm sorry. I'm so sorry."

There was silence.

Bria was unsure what to say. She had been calling Julia every day for a month, but this was the first time she picked up.

"Jules, I'm so…"

"Bria. He left again. He told me you were so drunk that night you had no idea what was happening. He took advantage of the situation. I fucking hate you, Bria!"

"I do, too."

More silence.

"What do we do now?" Bria asked.

"Do you still need help with your passport?"

"Jules, everything is different now. I just needed this, to hear your voice, to know that you're okay. I will work the rest of our lives trying to earn your forgiveness. I love you, Julia."

"Well, you can start by finding me another man. I can't go back to that asshole again." The girls giggled and for a moment, and Bria was reminded of a simpler time.

"Bri, are you okay? What is going on?"

Bria told Julia about the past month. She told her about the vendor altercation, her new business, not drinking, Devon and Antonio. She told her about the ransacked apartment and that they were looking for something from her father. She assumed it was a clue to where the family's wealth had gone. She left out the murder and attempted murder and murderers on the way.

"Does your aunt know what they're looking for?" Julia asked.

"No. Things are becoming a little more clear now. I think that's why she sent me to New York. What I didn't realize was that they were hiding me in plain sight."

"That makes so much sense. Even I couldn't find you. Do you think Nanny Delphina was somehow involved? Do you think she knew what they wanted? Maybe she took what they think you have?"

At that, Bria's mind spun. Where did her nanny go? Delphina was so steadfast, organizing Bria's belongings, maybe she was helping her aunt uncover clues as well? Maybe she found the thing of which everyone was now searching? But, no. Her nanny protected her. She remembered her nanny's son visiting. He was only a couple years older than Bria and he only spoke Italian. He still lived in Italy. Her nanny gave up her life to protect Bria's.

"No, she protected me. But I wonder, where did she go after I left for school?"

Bria was relieved to finally speak to Julia. They spoke until Bria's tiny burner phone started to flash of low battery. Bria needed that call. After that, everything would be easy.

Bria slipped into the hotel robe, exhausted from the cyclone of activity she managed in the past week. How she wished she hadn't left her mother's silk robe hanging on the door in her apartment. She was missing her old life desperately – not her old life in New York, no. Not advertising. She missed family and Julia was hers. Unfortunately, being with Bria right now was dangerous. She couldn't ask that of her best friend. Bria called room service.

"Do you have grappa?"

"No Miss Brigante, I'm sorry. May I interest you in a nice cognac or aperitif?"

"Bring me a Macallan twenty-five, neat."

"Of course, Miss Brigante. It will be right up."

Bria looked at her face in the mirror as she removed the remnants of makeup from her smooth skin. For the first time, she saw her mother. She saw Papà's eyes, but her face reminded her of her mother. Their faces were getting further away in her memory and she longed for the albums that were most likely ransacked and strewn across her Manhattan apartment. Bria traced her jawline with the warm rag. The glow from the sun reminded her of when Mama would return from Italy. She always looked relaxed, and beautiful, and wouldn't apply makeup for a week. Papà insisted this was how he loved her most, "without makeup so he could see her true beauty."

A tear fell from Bria's eye as the knock on the door came.

Bria grabbed her gun. She scolded herself for being lost in memory and letting her guard down. She moved the gun to her chest as she went to the door.

"Miss Brigante, it's me, Jesús. I have your nightcap, Señorita."

Did it sound like Jesús? Bria couldn't be cautious enough. She placed the gun in the robe pocket and crept toward the peephole.

"Señorita Brigante?" Jesús repeated.

Bria opened the door with her left hand to find Jesús smiling a big, toothy grin. Jesús was her regular room service waiter and – however it happened – she was happy to have him. He brought the small tray, adorned with a single hibiscus and two small chocolates. Bria chained the door after he entered, prepared to make an excuse if he had noticed.

As what had become the norm, Jesús didn't sing as he delivered her Macallan tonight. He simply asked, "No Brooklyn tonight, Señorita?"

"No, not tonight, Jesús."

"Señorita, do you need some extra towels or pillows this evening?'

"No Jesús, I'm fine, thank you."

Jesús gleamed over his shoulder as he placed the perfectly arranged tray on the table by the window. He craned his neck slightly as he looked out toward the beach.

"Jesús, is everything okay?" Bria asked.

"Oh, yes, yes, si, Señorita, si."

"Jesús?"

"Yes, Señorita Brigante? Can I do something for you?"

"Jesús, did you see someone?"

Jesús froze in his orthopedic black uniform shoes. He maybe tipped forty but the lines on his face showed a far older man. He was close to five feet tall with a stocky build and unruly black hair that was being unsuccessfully tamed with gobs of hair gel. No matter how he tried, his white uniform shirt escaped his pants from some direction on each delivery. Bria would giggle as she'd catch him walking by the mirror and, seeing his shirt untucked, he would start ranting, "Lo siento, Señorita. Lo siento mucho." He'd follow his apologies with a discreet tuck of his shirt as he scurried out the door – his orthopedics creating so much static as he dragged them that his hair would have stood on end be it not for the pound of hair gel. Jesús was, in a word, adorable. Bria sometimes ordered room service late at night just for his smile. His wrinkles told one story, but his smile another. Tonight, he smiled but his eyes spoke a new language.

Bria continued as a whisper, "Jesús, it's okay, you're safe. Did someone approach you?"

SANTIAGO

Santiago started Tuesday. Santiago was a self-proclaimed Dominican Italian who made Bria laugh as much as he frightened her with his steely gaze. He was not the largest man she interviewed, but the quickest. She liked that he practiced Jiu jitsu. But more so? She liked that he was smart. Santiago would be her body guard, but she would also spend more time with him than anyone else. She immediately thought of Uncle Louie. Uncle Louie, Bria wouldn't learn until his burial, wasn't a Brigante. She had never asked. Uncle Louie and Papà were inseparable. He drank wine with the family at dinner and drove Papà everywhere. He was always present at meetings and would never take a glass of wine when Bria was asked to pour some in a business meeting.

So many pieces of the puzzle were falling into place, and Bria had just hired a Dominican-Italian Uncle Louie.

Santiago was six foot two and had a lean build with strong shoulders. His clothes had a better drape than the typical islander and his tanned skin and dark hair made him blend in just enough with the natives. It was when Santiago spoke that you knew he was different. He spoke fluent Spanish and fluent Italian, but when he spoke English it was the Italian you detected. He had wavy dark hair that held its fair share of pomade, and his five o-clock shadow accentuated the age in his sharp eyes. Bria guessed Santiago to be in his mid-thirties, maybe forty. In Santiago's business, there was no room for I-9's and proof of identification. Your proof was your instinct. If your instinct was wrong, Bria imagined she'd need to hire a bigger and smarter

Santiago to eliminate the one she inadvertently trusted.

By the end of day one, Bria was sure she had hired the right man for the job. Her curiosity was put to rest when she asked about his family.

"I had a family once, Miss Brigante, but they are now gone." Santiago's eyes lowered, and Bria didn't need to ask more questions.

"I lost my family, too. I'm sorry."

Santiago looked up at Bria, his eyebrow raised, acknowledging that he had done his homework already on his new boss.

"I think our situations are the same." Santiago said. He continued, "You lost your Papà, I lost my children. We both lost others, we both loved the others as strongly, but our hearts want revenge for the ones we need."

"Yes, Santiago. Yes."

Santiago couldn't help but look at Bria like a daughter, although she was much older than his own. He had lost his own daughter to gang violence in Santo Domingo. He had lost his wife and son as well. They were looking for Santiago but attacked and tortured his family instead. Watching his family's attackers die a slow death didn't help Santiago heal. He was left hoping he could have watched them burn in hell as well. "An eye for an eye," he'd tell himself as he prayed to God for forgiveness. "They are yours now to forgive, Dios mío."

When Santiago heard about this beautiful woman protecting herself and then taking over the beach, he wasn't sure if he could help her or if she would become his next enemy. In Santo Domingo, Santiago wasn't a killer. He was in the wrong place at the wrong time. Desperate times made him do things that he would regret, but he needed to feed his family. His gift was knowing all the right people as well as he had known all the wrong ones. He had grown up in the Dominican. When the island economy turned, losing his job meant turning to other means to support his family. There was nothing more important than family. Santiago's own father had come to the Dominican Republic from Italy to follow a wealthy real estate developer. The man was incorrigible, but his father knew that by following him here, he could give his family a life they couldn't have imagined on the southern coast of Italy.

Family meant everything to Santiago, and he would learn from his friend Riccardo at the Blooming Sands that it meant the same to his new boss. When he met Bria, he knew he had made the right decision. And now, after spending just a day with her, Bria Brigante already felt like family.

As it turned out, Santiago knew everyone of importance. He knew airport security, police, mayors, and municipal councils. He also knew several seedier characters, which might come in handier than Bria originally expected. As it turned out, tourists in almost every resort were looking for a safe way to procure drugs. The Caribe Resort asked for X and opioids while the Blooming Sands wanted high-end edibles. This was a part of the business Devon would need to be shielded from, but it made Santiago a perfect fit.

MAMA

Bria's marketing mockups sold events and products before Devon could finish his pitch. Unfortunately for Devon, drugs were a part of the package.

"Mood enhancers," Bria called them. Although Bria was cautious to exclude him from the less desirable profits, how would Devon explain his new partner to Dylan Lancaster?

Devon was changing, and the thought of the senior Lancaster jumped out of his head faster than it jumped in most days. Santiago was a nice fit for the team and allowed Devon to relax significantly and focus on growing his division of Brigante Enterprises. He had barely thought about his father over the past week and his sole focus had been building his new empire with his partner. Bria had given Devon the roadmap, but it was Devon who connected with three other large chains and was helping the pair take over multiple islands.

Bria, Devon, and Santiago walked the beach back toward Blooming Sands. The last few days had produced results that far exceeded their expectations and the conversation was so intense they no longer noticed the sea breeze and the soft sand that had become their office. Bria was telling Devon he needed to incorporate and create a formal business as Santiago answered his phone and dropped several paces behind.

"Si… si… cuando? … Donde están ahora?… Gracias, amigo, te deberé"

Santiago quickened his pace, "Mama, excuse me Mama!"

"What did you call me, Santiago?" Bria looked at him in shock.

"I'm sorry, Miss Brigante. This is what the islanders call you. Mama. I forgot. Miss Bri..."

Bria cut him off, "Why do they call me Mama, Santiago?"

"They call you Mama because you take care of everyone but you're..." Santiago stopped mid-sentence, trying to retract his words.

"I'm what, Santiago?" Devon smirked as Bria grilled him, thankful it wasn't him. Bria may be twenty-six, she may be inexplicably beautiful, but she was none of those things when she was focused. She was fierce. She was frightening.

"I'm sorry. I should have said no thing. Miss Brigante, I just got a call..." Again, Bria interrupted.

"Santiago, my family is my blood. You are now my family. Do you have any siblings, Santiago? Do you tell them the shitty stuff? Of course, you do. It's fun to piss off a sibling, that's what family does. Piss me off before I disown you, Santiago. Tell me now." Bria didn't laugh. Her voice was steady. Even though he had just started working mere days ago, Santiago knew better than to be quiet.

"They call you Mama because you take care of everyone, but also because the only one a thug is afraid of is his mama." Santiago seemed smaller to Devon than he had minutes ago.

"I like that," was all Bria said on the matter. "Now, what was your phone call about?"

"Miss Brigante, my contacts in Santiago told me three men were asking about you and someone named Julia Strichorn. No one told them no thing, Miss Brigante." There were slight pauses between each of his words for effect. "No one told them no thing. Don't worry."

"Julia." Bria was silent and then, "Oh my God, Julia."

Devon almost screeched and his voice quickened with each word, "What? Who's Julia? Who cares who Julia is? Three men are here to kill you and they probably have guns. Big guns!" His panic knocked Bria out of her shock.

"Devon, there is a light side and a dark side to our business. I think it's important to keep you on the light side." Bria looked at him with pity.

"I'm sorry, Bria. I lost my mind. We need to get you out of here." Devon responded.

"I agree, Mama," said Santiago.

"NO." Bria was abrupt and firm. *"Quando cacciate; lascia che il gioco venga da te.* We wait for them. Santiago, have your friends tell them where I am. Tell them Julia Strichorn is here with me."

"Mama, are you sure?" Santiago pushed back carefully. He could tell Bria liked the sound of Mama, but he wasn't sure why. She was at least ten years younger than him and he was sure she had a physique that never gave birth.

"Yes," answered Bria.

Santiago went to call his friends when Bria yelled back to him, "And Santiago, I need someone like you who can go to New York."

"Yes, Mama."

Devon's head spun. He felt like he had stepped in a Grand Prix race car a week ago and hasn't stopped gripping the safety bar since. He wasn't in control, but he was part of the ride, and it was exhilarating.

Devon and Bria continued walking while Santiago fell ten steps behind to make his call. As they walked, Bria sensed the anxiety in Devon, "You okay, Devs?"

"Was this your life before your family was killed?" He wanted to suck the words back as soon as they left his lips.

"No. My life was safe and beautiful and wonderful. We always had people around. Of course, I was seventeen and far from naïve; I knew what Papà was doing."

Devon caught his breath as she called him Papà. This woman captivated him. She unnerved him. Without trying, she made him feel small in her presence. Everything he thought he knew thirty days ago had diminished; he now knew how much he still had to learn. Bria had something he had never known. Bria had power that was not given from position but was worn like an invisible crown. Moments like these, when she allowed glimpses of her humanity, these moments gave her more power. Devon was silent as Bria continued her story.

"Papà let me sit in on many meetings. Of course, business was usually completed before I was allowed to join them, but I learned as much sitting outside his office door as I did when I was invited in. I loved him so much. He was my life. I wanted so much to make him proud."

"Bria, look around," Devon said, "Wherever your father is, he has got a glass of Macallan and he's watching you continue his legacy. He's proud, all right. I couldn't imagine a father prouder." Devon thought of his own father. Had he ever been proud of Devon, or had Devon's accomplishments always been a result of Dylan Lancaster's puppetry?

Devon gently touched her arm. It seemed strangely forbidden. Her gaze was down, but slowly raised as she looked at Devon.

"Devon, tell me about your father."

Devon was speechless. Compared with what he had learned about Bria, he was suddenly feeling childish. There was no loss. There was no loyalty. Devon had a family who was still here, still supporting him, and still offering him a world ninety-nine percent of the population would never understand. Devon now saw that he was being too pig-headed to accept it.

"My story makes me sound like a spoiled rich kid trying to piss off his father."

Bria laughed, "Well, aren't you?"

"I didn't think so last week."

Bria smiled. "Maybe, Devs, you're just not communicating what you truly want to accomplish to your father? From what I've read about the Lancaster story, you have more in common with him than you think."

"You read..." Devon started.

"Don't be coy. You knew I would. I don't go into business with just anyone." Her wisdom marred her expression.

"Are we in business, or do I work for you?" Devon asked.

"Devs, we have separate businesses, but we will make millions and millions together."

Devon knew this was her way of protecting him.

"Bella! Bella! Bella, Bria! Over here my love!" Bria looked up as Antonio approached them from the water. He pulled his long, wet hair into a bun and tied it with a hair tie as he approached the couple. The water moved down his ribbed stomach like a waterfall. As he moved within twenty feet, Santiago pushed his own imposing figure between Antonio and Bria.

"No, no, Santiago. This is the man I told you about." Bria said protectively of Antonio. They kissed both cheeks and Antonio started babbling about the hawk sanctuary.

"Antonio, slow down, what are you saying?" This was unlike Antonio.

"Come with me, Bella. I want to show you the property again. I think you can build a beautiful home."

"Antonio, I'm not sure where this is coming from, but now is not a good time."

"Please, Bella. This property is beautiful. Let your men take care of your business. Come with me." Antonio almost pleaded. Bria changed before Antonio's eyes. The men could see her eyes darkening, the look of betrayal crossing her expression.

"Antonio, you know, don't you?"

"No, Bella. What are you talking about? I just want to spend an afternoon with you looking at the beautiful waves."

"Antonio. I'm taking care of this. How did you know?" Everyone on the beach knew time would stand still until Antonio answered her question. Her tone always said far more than her words.

"Then you go, Bella. Let us take care of this problem," Antonio conceded.

"Antonio, how do you know? Who sent you here? How do you know me?" Bria ignored his plea and made it clear she would wait for his answer. Santiago stepped forward again, closer to Antonio.

Antonio finally responded, "I am from the family. I will explain later, but we need to get you to safety pronto, Bella."

Bria stepped back.

"What family?"

"Your family, Bella," Antonio answered.

"I have no family."

"This is where you're wrong. But there is no time to explain, we need to keep you safe."

Santiago looked ready to launch. Bria's hand slowly moved out to the side, open, as if the sheer force field around it was enough to hold back Santiago's two-hundred-and-twenty-pound frame. Santiago looked at Bria silently and awaited her next order.

Bria locked eyes with Antonio and seethed, "I am not running anywhere. We called them to us."

"Bria, Bella, these are very dangerous men. They will do whatever it takes to get what they want. Bella, per favore. Concedimi questo onore."

"I will meet them." Bria answered simply and then turned to continue her march back to the Blooming Sands.

When the four reached the hotel, Bria stopped.

"Devon, you must go. You can't be near this. Go to that cute HR girl's room. She'll be thrilled."

"No, I'm staying to help." Devon stood strong.

Ignoring him, Bria continued, "Stay in her room until you hear from us. You can't be a part of this, it's bad for business. Devon, go! You must honor your father as well."

Devon stared, speechless. Antonio silently nodded to him, assuring him it was the right thing to do.

"Santiago, take Antonio and fetch José and Leandro. Bring these men to me when they arrive."

"No, Bella, let me stay with you," Antonio pleaded.

"Non disonorarmi." Antonio bowed at Bria's retort. He motioned toward Santiago to lead the way, leaving Bria alone, unguarded on the beach in front of the Blooming Sands Resort.

HISTORY

Papà hated Jonathan Reilly. Worse than the fact that he would be dating his daughter was the fact that he was Irish.

"Ah, Bella! Reilly? You know his father is probably a potato farmer, no? Do you want to marry a potato farmer, Bella?" Bria would be enraged and want to date him more. Bella knew how to push the limits with Papà, and Jonathan Reilly was one of the ways. It was Jonathan Reilly who saved her life, though.

Uncle Louie didn't want Papà to go out.

"Not tonight, Papà. The natives are restless. I don't have a good feeling."

"Non disonorarmi! My daughter wants to go to 'The Lion King' and we're going! Make sure everything is ready for us when we arrive."

That was the last order Bria heard her father give.

Curfew was at midnight because it was prom. Normally it was ten-thirty p.m. Familiar men drove the limo that escorted the four young lovers that evening. Bria had recognized them as Papà's men as soon as they arrived with the poshly decorated, white stretch limousine. The driver knew everyone's name and addressed them appropriately. His passenger in the other seat in front was quick to open doors and bow gracefully as the young revelers bounded in and out. When at the prom, the passenger with his matching black suit and valet's hat stood amongst the balloons near the entrance, his eyes constantly darting about the room. Papà's men were never inconspicuous to Bria, but no one else seemed to ever notice them.

As the tall dark figure fought the ever-moving balloons, Bria couldn't help but giggle as he swiped them away in annoyance or one would cling to the back of his head with static. Bria was used to bodyguards. Her father could be overprotective, and she and her sister were constantly toying with them. When they were younger, the girls would split up or dart around the corner to see if they could lose them. When they'd return home, Papà would be waiting with his fist on the big desk and his office door open, waiting to scold them. Bria wasn't interested in the bodyguard that evening, she was interested in being kissed by Jonathan Reilly. That was, until the bodyguard changed her plans.

It was ten-forty-seven p.m. when the man with the valet hat rushed onto the dance floor and grabbed Bria by the arm.

"You need to come with me, it's urgent," he said.

"No!" Bria started to disarm him with a jiu-jitsu move when he stopped her hand.

"Bria, it's Papà. Something's wrong."

She no longer fought him but ran with him to the waiting car. Jonathan Reilly stood standing in the middle of the dance floor in shock. Bria didn't look back.

Bria stepped into the back of the car while Papà's man entered the back with her. The car started screeching out of the driveway before the man had time to shut the door behind him. The driver was taking orders from someone on the phone and barking orders back to the man sitting beside her, his gun drawn.

"What is happening?!?" Bria demanded.

The two men ignored her.

"Damn it! Is Papà okay? Talk to me!" She screamed, enraged. It was so loud both men stopped talking and silence fell in the car. Bria lowered her voice, but her father's tone erupted, "You will tell me now. What is going on and where is my father?"

The men were too shocked to answer. Their eyes stared at her, unable to break their gaze. At that, the driver slammed on the brakes and the stretch limousine skidded through the busy

New Jersey intersection. Bria didn't flinch.

"What happened?" Bria repeated calmly.

The man beside her spoke quietly. "We don't know. There was an accident. We think someone tried to attack your father. We need to get you to safety."

"My father, or my family?"

"Bria." The man struggled to continue.

"I want to talk to Uncle Louie. Get Uncle Louie on the phone!"

The man with the hat simply responded, "Louie was with Papà, too."

Bria looked over at Papà's journal. Was it enough to help her through what was still to come?

FANGS

Bria took her time getting ready. She couldn't help but remember that night. She wondered what Papà was thinking before he left the house. She opened her father's journal and read the quotes he had written. *A carne di lupo, zanne di cane.* She knew this from her father. For wolf flesh; dog fangs. It was time to be tough. Whenever someone would visit who Papà didn't like, he'd turn to Uncle Louie and say, "*A carne di lupo, zanne di cane.*" She wasn't surprised to see it in his journal, but what she understood when she first read it had changed. It was not about getting tougher when life was tough, it was him telling her that sometimes she'd need to rely on her fangs to fight. To eat wolf flesh, a dog must use his fangs. Let them see your fangs. Don't just get tougher, be tougher. She couldn't rely on others. Bria would sharpen her own fangs before returning to the beach.

As if he knew, Ricardo had reserved Bria's favorite cabana. He had drawn the side panels for privacy and filled it with a feast. Bria noticed a four-foot-tall blue urn from the hotel was now placed oddly at the back corner of the cabana. She couldn't help but wonder how Ricardo might have moved it alone, or why? Even empty it was beautiful. Next to it sat Ricardo's podium and a small fern artistically staged, as if to make the urn look less out of place. It didn't.

Ricardo welcomed Bria to her cabana and handed her a cool towelette. She sat quietly, her long hair flowing elegantly over her smart dress. Her skin was radiant with its sun-kissed glow. She wore her Saint Laurent glasses in her shaded enclave and waited.

Bria sat contemplatively, patiently, and with her gun and the memories of her family readied beside her.

THE VISITORS

Devon couldn't even remember the HR manager's name, yet Bria seemed to know there was a connection between them. As he walked toward her office, he wondered how he would get her to her room, or better yet, keep her out of her room. He wanted to wait to hear from Bria there without the kind woman's maddening babble. His legs felt heavy as he took the final steps through the lobby to her office. This is not what he wanted to be doing. He wanted to turn around and go back to Bria. How could he leave her alone with men who had every intention of killing her? Honor. That's the only thing he understood of her conversation with Antonio. Honor was what made him turn away. Honor made him bow to her. Bria was right, if Devon looked to be involved, it would immediately hurt his business – their business. Bria Brigante had given him a business. Why was it she could hand him a business, but from his own father, it wasn't palatable? Bria needed Devon's good name to move faster. Bria Brigante needed Devon, and, oddly, Devon Lancaster needed her.

Devon opened the door to the HR office to find it empty apart from the payroll clerk. He looked at the name on the manager's desk. "Where's Donna?"

"Oh, I'm sorry, all the HR managers are at a meeting in Miami with Bloomfield Corp. Donna won't be back until Monday. Is there something I can help you with, Devon?" He was caught off guard that she knew his name.

"No, no. It can wait."

"Okay, Devon, I'll make sure Donna knows you were asking

about her," she sang. She obviously knew about their date.

"No need, I don't want to ruin the surprise." Devon hoped this would keep the girl quiet for a while. "Which room is hers? I want to slip something under her door."

She giggled. "Ohhh, she's in the management suites. It's room two hundred six-one."

"Thank you," he looked at her name plate, "Amayah."

Devon almost sprinted to his room to retrieve the master key set and then back to the elevator. He pushed the elevator button, impatiently eyeing the stairs and wondering if he could beat the elevator down nineteen flights. Finally, the door chimed, and he stepped in. The ride down seemed just as long. The time from the airport to the hotel took an hour, so there wasn't much time.

What was he doing? The thought pummeled his brain. How could he help?

Devon walked quickly toward room two sixty-one. He was frustrated to see it on the front side of the building, far from any beach view. He fumbled through the keys to find the right floor. He finally opened the door and entered the room.

Ordinarily, Devon couldn't imagine trespassing like this. As he entered the tiny room, that was his last thought. He walked through Donna's neat little suite, barely noticing books on finding men and a small array of lined up fragrances. Devon rushed to the balcony and stepped out. He quickly stepped back in. Did they know what he looked like? What did Vinny know before he died? Did he tell his boss? Obviously, Bria thought they knew of him. She also seemed to know these men would not be deterred by the passkey secured penthouse floor he normally enjoyed. Devon pulled the sheers over the balcony door and peered through to the grounds. As he scoured the view for holes in the foliage, he could just make out the hotel entrance and a piece of the driveway. Just then his phone rang.

"Are you all right?" Devon almost shouted.

"Buddy, what are you talking about? It's me, Max." Max

Bloomfield III responded.

Shocked that he made such a stupid mistake, he quickly corrected, "Max, I'm sorry. My mother and father are at it again. I thought it was her. We just hung up. Sorry buddy."

"No problem. Is everything okay?"

"Yea, yea. You know, my mother can be a bit of a drama queen," Devon responded, catching his breath as he talked.

"Are you okay? Sounds like you just ran a marathon."

"Oh yeah, yeah. Just got off the treadmill. What's going on?" Devon looked at himself in the mirror as he talked. Calm down, calm down.

"Hey, I was just checking in. Sounds like you and my father had a pretty productive golf game? I'm surprised you didn't call me."

"I'm sorry, things just happened so fast. I didn't expect Bria to be sitting in the club when we finished."

"So, I take it you don't think she's a mafia princess trying to overthrow the Bloomfield empire?" Max asked quite seriously.

"No, as a matter of fact, she's damn brilliant. I was surprised." Devon was sincere.

"So, she's not Papà Brigante's daughter?" Max continued.

"Well, she is, actually. We had a pretty long conversation about her family. It's a long story but let talk about it next time you're here. To sum it up, I don't think we have anything to worry about." Devon said this as he stared at the front entrance of the hotel nervously.

"So, you're staying there?" Max seemed incredulous.

"For a while. She inspired me to start a business, and you're my first client." Devon was too focused on the entrance to even crack a smile as he said it.

"So, I guess you found your mermaid," teased Max.

"Huh. I guess I did. Hey, can I call you back? I need to jump in the shower, but I want to talk to you about renting a room long term here, until I find something more permanent."

"You're like family. Don't worry. Stay as long as you need it."

"Thanks, Max. I'll call you later."

Devon hung up. "You're like family." They had used that phrase with each other many times over the year. They'd called each other "brother," they'd been at each other's homes, vacationed together... but they weren't family. Family meant something different to Devon now. His family was sitting in a beach cabana with a gun ready to take on three armed men while wearing high heels.

Just then, he watched three men drive up in a rental car. He watched for golf clubs. None. There was one duffle bag they retrieved from the trunk. They were here.

THE CABANA

Bria sat alone in the cabana Ricardo had prepared for her, oddly comforted by the thin, athletic man standing at the podium he had placed behind it. What had compelled him to rearrange the beach? Had he known they'd be coming today?

It was quiet on the beach today. The beach vendors were all assigned to hotels and events so they no longer littered the beach. It was just after lunchtime, so the tourists were all napping or partaking in Bria's afternoon craft shows she had organized at the resorts. It was hard to believe what she had accomplished in a little over a week. There were still many hotels to visit and more business to generate for the vendors on this beach, but right now, Bria needed to be focused on her immediate problem.

Unfortunately, her problem was on its way to this cabana.

The placement of her cabana was perfect. Unless you craned your neck, you couldn't see in past the palms. Bria was surprised by how large the cabana was. When the side shades were drawn, it really gave a different perspective and she wondered if she could hold meetings here, like her father had in his big office. Bria tried to stay focused, but fear continued to distract her with random thoughts. She thought about building her home in the hawk sanctuary at the top of the hill. She thought about which island to build her business on next – although her plans were partially dictated by the new Blooming Sands contract. Most importantly, she thought about what her father would be thinking about right now if it was him sitting here, and not her.

Grappa, she thought and laughed at herself.

She couldn't imagine Papà nervous. Papà was fearless. But was he? Did Devon and Antonio and Santiago think she was nervous? No. They saw the cool Brigante front.

Bria looked at her burner phone. Twenty minutes, she surmised. Twenty minutes and her nerves of steel would certainly be tested. Was she willing to die for what they wanted? Yes. Bria would die avenging her family name. Bria looked to the sea.

"Papà, are you with me? Papà, I need you with me. I miss you, Papà. I'm so sorry Papà. I'm sorry I didn't listen, I'm sorry I let you down, I'm sorry if I embarrassed you… I need you with me today. Give me the strength to be a Brigante and protect what is ours and avenge your murder. Papà, help me avenge your murder."

Bria paused.

"Damn those bastards! Papà, help me take them down."

GUNS AND A SERRATED KNIFE

Santiago took the lead and Antonio followed. He called José and Leandro, who were out collecting on the beach. Santiago and José took the front doors, Antonio and Leandro the beach entrance. They couldn't be sure the men looking for Bria wouldn't recognize Antonio. He needed to stay out of sight. Seeing Antonio too soon might scare them off, so Antonio and Leandro took the back entrance, where they were least likely to show.

Forty minutes into their watch, the call came. The three men just arrived at the front door of the Blooming Sands in a four-door rental sedan.

There was no questioning their intentions, or who they were. They all had dark hair and dark brown eyes. The one with the dyed, jet-black hair that thinned slightly on the top, was the oldest and wore a suit. Despite his age, he looked strong and angry. His partner had a brand-new Tommy Bahama shirt and shorts that still held creases from where they were folded on the shelf. He was the largest of the three and as he bent to pick up the duffel bag, you could make out a hard object tucked into his belt at his lower back. The third was the youngest with tufts of black hair pouring out of his wife-beating tank top that was partially hidden under a similarly creased Tommy Bahama ensemble. There was hair everywhere. It framed his head and stopped where he shaved it. It was so thick on his arms that it was flattened by his shirt sleeve and curled around it where they met. All three men shared the same style in gold jewelry and it adorned their necks, their wrists, and their pinkies. Watching them get their bag and give the valet orders about where they wanted their car parked made every head turn as their abrupt voices and truncated style of speaking announced the arrival of a foreign entity to the posh resort.

As Santiago, José and Leandro got into position, Antonio made his entrance into the lobby.

"Fellas! It's been a long time, no?" Antonio greeted the three men as they took their first steps into the lobby.

"What are you doing here?" the old one rumbled.

"Oh, gentlemen, is this the kind of greeting you give me? What has it been, nine years?"

"Where is she, Tony?"

"Well, well, you must first call me by my proper name. It's An-to-ni-o. You understand? Antonio." Antonio kept his hands in plain sight so they wouldn't be tempted to touch their weapons. As he goaded them, Santiago, José and Leandro stepped behind each one, grabbing their arms firmly behind them. Santiago used his foot to push the duffle bag to the ground beneath the large man and almost simultaneously, Bria's team pushed guns discreetly into their sides.

"Let me introduce you to my friends, gentlemen." Antonio went to each man and took their weapons and patted them down.

Antonio walked over to the older man with the dyed hair and said, "Arturo. It's so nice to see you. Arturo, your tour guide for the afternoon will be Leandro. Leandro eats small children of our enemies for lunch. You understand, Artie?"

"Dis ain't the fucking dating game, Tony. Where's the kid?" Arturo tried to lunge toward Antonio but Leandro's grip allowed barely a movement.

"Tch, tch, tch, Artie. Are you stuck?" Antonio guffawed as he watched Arturo struggle against the giant Leandro. Antonio continued. "You have not seen this kid – as you call her – lately, no?"

At that, the big man started to grumble as he tried to pry his hands from Santiago. "Where's Brianna?" the big man demanded.

"Ha! It looks like you're in no position to bark orders, big man. Did you see the size of my friend, Santiago? You are a giant in comparison, but it seems like the mighty has fallen to the mightier mouse." Antonio wasn't sure who this comment infuriated more – the big man or Santiago.

"Watch it. Tony." Santiago said provocatively.

"Ah, my brother, you know this man is one foot bigger than you, no?"

"Watch it, Antonio. I would hate to have to take my anger out on my captive." Santiago tightened his hold as he said the words.

"You see, gentlemen, we are family. I make-a my brother mad and he takes it out on you. Ima so sorry, Santi." Antonio enjoyed the game. As he moved to pat down the hairy man, Antonio said, "José, how would you like to be introduced to this big hairy man?"

"As the Terminator." José laughed at himself as he said it.

"He he he. Very good my brother. You are the Terminator. You might want to be the ex-Terminator."

"Why's that?" José complied.

"Well, your captive has so much, how do you call it, fur? I would be worries about fleas."

At that Bria's men laughed in unison.

Antonio continued, "Now that I know you have no weapons, I shall escort you back to— what do you call her? Oh yes, 'the kid.'"

Antonio retrieved the duffle bag from beneath Santiago's foot and added the newly collected guns to the zipped arsenal.

"Now, gentlemen, we will bring you to Mama. This is what we call her." Antonio smiled.

"Mama? What the fuck? Is this a fucking joke?" the hairy one smarted. At that, José tightened his grip. "Merda!"

José silently smiled.

"Right this way. However with that language, I'm not so sure I can still call you gentlemen. Artie, I think you need to teach these new ones some manners." Antonio walked without looking back at the men and led them through the lobby to the cabana.

Ricardo, standing outside the canvas wall, nodded as the men entered the cabana.

"I see you've found me," said Bria calmly and without standing. The three men stood captive in the hands of her henchmen. Antonio moved to the seat next to her and pulled his gun from his back. "I prefer my gun, it's much quieter," he quipped.

"What is it you want, gentlemen?" Bria asked calmly.

"You see, she doesn't know you like I do, she still calls you gentlemen." Antonio quipped.

None of the men answered.

Bria continued, "Well, it seems a shame to come all this way and not get what you want."

"You know what we want." The old man with the dyed hair grunted.

"Yes, and why should I give it to you?" Bria played with them.

"You have no choice. If you don't give it to us, we'll find it, but I guarantee you won't live long enough to see what we do with it," chimed the hairy thug.

"Gentlemen, apparently, you don't see what I see." Bria smiled.

It was then, the oldest man reached behind him and flipped Leandro to the ground while kicking José. Leandro fell to the ground long enough for the man to punch Santiago and help the big man free himself from Santiago's grip. José held tight to the hairy man with the wife beater until the big man clocked him in the head at a speed immeasurable to human eyes.

JUST IN TIME

Devon couldn't allow them to protect Bria alone. He ran from the room and to the stairwell. He could not listen to this order from his new business partner, he had to help her. He finally had a plan, he was finally excited about something, he was finally scared. This was all because of Bria Brigante, and he would not let anything happen to her.

Devon sped down the stairs to find the main floor locked. Why the fuck was it locked? He banged on the door furiously, no one responded. He used all his might and pushed the door with all the force he could muster. He kicked it. He rammed it. It wouldn't budge. He ran back to the second floor and pounded on the elevator button. As it opened, it was crowded with guests. Devon wedged his way in while trying to stay calm.

As the door opened, Devon pounced out, trying to remain calm and not drawing any attention to himself. He walked through the kitchen entrance and greeted the group with a simple "Hey!" As he was welcomed by his co-workers, he asked, "Gil, I'm going to borrow a knife to open that coconut I told you about. I gotta figure out how those kids on the beach do that." The sous chef smiled and shook his head, "Sure, brothah."

No one seemed to notice the sweat beading on Devon's forehead. No one noticed how fast he was walking through the kitchen. Behind the swinging doors to the culinary epicenter, everything was status quo.

"You going to the bonfire tonight, brothah?"

"Yeah, I'll be dare man. When you going?"

"Devon, you comin' brothah? You too fancy for us now that

you moved up to dee penthouse?"

"I'll be there," Devon said obligingly as he quickly grabbed a knife and wrapped it in a kitchen towel. He held his hand up in thanks as he scurried out the door and headed toward the beach. He walked toward Bria's regular spot. Her cabana seemed more out of view than usual. Someone had moved an empty urn and plant outside of it. As he closed in on the cabana, he noticed the canvas walls moving. Bodies were being pushed against the walls. He quickened his pace. As he got closer, he noticed damp splattered dots on the canvas. Was it blood? The movement stopped.

Devon could only think the worst. As he closed in, he heard a man yell.

"Who was it?"

Could he take on three thugs with one knife? He had to try.

In the cabana, the six men were entangled closely, leaving no shot for Antonio. Santiago took a pinky ring under his left eye, tearing away the flesh and splattering blood on the cabana and his assailant. Leandro was easily grounded a second time while José struggled to regain control of his charge. The cabana walls were being tossed about by the brawling men while Antonio struggled to find a shot. Bria remained calm, sitting on the settee, watching. Antonio tried to kick the big one away from Santiago long enough to get a shot from behind but the big man was no match for the average-size playboy. It was then that Bria noticed a muscular, tan arm reach around José. The strong arm slid his serrated blade across the hairy man's neck as blood oozed from the deep gap he was carving. The hairy man now wore a red wife beater and collapsed in his own pool of blood. As the large one turned toward the newcomer, Antonio placed a bullet in the back of his large head, his frontal lobe exploding through the exit wound and splattering Leandro. Santiago subdued the old man with dyed hair. He held his arm out, keeping their newest ally from slicing another neck.

"Who was it?" Santiago barked. Antonio moved closer and moved his gun to his head, but the knife was already positioned near the man's jugular vein.

Bria rose.

"Now, what were you saying?" she smiled politely.

As Devon rounded the entrance to the cabana, one thug stood. He was surrounded by Antonio, Santiago, José, Leandro and— Ricardo. The waiter held a knife to the thug's neck as Santiago held him, facing Bria.

"Now, what were you saying?" Devon heard her say.

Devon walked toward the palm trees and picked up a coconut that had fallen to the ground. He sat on the sand, his back on the tree, and opened his kitchen towel. He heard a little scuffling, but it was clear Bria was not going to give. It was underneath the beautiful palm tree with a fresh coconut in his hand that Devon first heard the words, come from Bria's mouth, "Ricorda il mio cognome." It was followed by a quiet spit of a silencer, and Devon saw the body fall against the wall of the cabana. She must have stepped over his corpse to leave.

"I told you to stay in Donna's room." Bria was cool as she spoke.

"I couldn't."

"I know."

"Are you okay?"

"Of course."

Antonio stepped out of the cabana and walked up to the couple, brushing off his hands as if he was dusting sand off his shorts. "Ah, Devon, you came too late. You missed all of the fun."

"I'm sorry I couldn't help, I would have been there earlier, but the stairwell door was locked." Bria and Antonio looked at each other and laughed. Devon continued, "Are you going to let me in on your little joke?"

"You see, Devon. I was a' once like you. I didn't understand I needed to listen to my Mama. I locked the door, I knew you'd come back. You just don't understand family yet. You will, you will." With that, Antonio and Bria laughed more while Antonio patted Devon on the back.

"Welcome to the family, Devon." Bria kissed him on the cheek.

"Not two cheeks?" asked Devon.

"Two cheeks say hello and good-bye, one cheek means I care. Now protect me with that big knife of yours while we walk the beach. Those guys are going to busy for a while."

"Of course. What are they going to do with— never mind. I don't think I want to know."

"It's better that way, trust me Devon." Bria assured him.

"Did you find out what they wanted from you?" asked Devon.

"No. Just that they think I have it."

"And Ricardo? I had no idea, Bria." Devon shook his head as the words came out of his mouth. "Is he family as well?"

"He is now, I suppose. Ricardo has a family, that's who he was really protecting. When I came to Blooming Sands, I made him a lot of money and Ricardo started taking care of me. It was his way of taking care of his family as well. He had noticed Vinny as well. Of everyone, I suppose Ricardo had the best view of me and of him. He also recognized Antonio watching me. He appointed himself my protector. He saw you bring me to the hotel and watched Vinny follow us, and he followed Vinny."

"So, Ricardo was your hero in the elevator." Devon concluded.

"Yes."

"Why didn't you tell me?" asked Devon.

"I didn't trust you yet. There was something you weren't telling me, and I didn't want Ricardo to lose his job. Ricardo is not a killer, he's a hero." Bria stated.

"But he's killed now at least two men. Maybe he is?"

"No, I am his Mama. I look out for him, and he looks out for me. He's a hero."

"You're twenty-six. It's funny to hear you called Mama."

"It's a sign of respect. Besides, this is my family now, Devon," Bria replied.

They walked quietly past the shanties. Unlike two weeks ago, the vendors showered her with love and excitement. Several ran up to her and thanked her. Another told her that her show at the Hard Rock Hotel this afternoon made her more money in one day than she made in two weeks. Another showed her a new necklace she designed with Larimar and named it "Mama." It had two curved stones, one smaller than the other. that nested against each other to form a pendant. The larger stone seemed to hold the smaller stone. The curves made it elegant and a perfect homage to a mother.

Bria said, "This is beautiful, I am honored. You can sell that at Caribe for seventy-five, but if you find a smoother and more robust metal to set it in, I bet you could sell it for five hundred at Blooming Sands." The vendor ran away elated. At that, a small boy ran up to Bria with three coconuts.

"Are you going to juggle coconuts for me, Rico?"

"No. Mama, I want to do a show. I want to carve coconuts for the tourists and then we let them buy the coconuts from me after."

"Ohhh," Bria said, "Why don't you bring me three coconuts and carve them for me tomorrow. I would like to see your show." The boy ran off with his coconuts as fast as he could but stopped thirty feet away. He looked at Bria and dropped his coconuts.

The young entrepreneur stood in the sand looking at them both, and then in a flash, he ran as fast as he could to Bria and gave her legs and torso an incredibly hug.

"Thank you, Mama. Thank you!"

It was remarkable. The beach was clean of vendors. As they walked past various hotels, sometimes three vendors would be at small tables under the palm trees awaiting guests at their pop-up store. Some were in sets of three inside of the resort or near the pool. When they saw Bria, they always waved.

Bria and Devon continued to walk the beach until there were no more hotels and the beach grew more deserted. Devon closed his eyes to suck in the warm, scented air. It was then that he heard a choir of voices behind them.

"Mama!"

"Bria!"

"Mister!"

"Run!"

"No!"

"Mama!"

They looked back to find forty islanders chasing them up the beach, yelling. As Bria looked back, a man wearing linen pants and a button-down shirt pulled out his gun toward Bria. Bria reached between her legs to grab her own gun and the man shouted, "Don't touch it!" Devon looked at the knife in his hand. Should he throw it? How could he help her? Devon stepped in front of Bria.

"I'll blow a hole through the both of you," he said dryly. "Where is he, Bria?"

"Who?" Bria asked, pushing Devon aside and stepping toward the man.

"Papà. Where is he?"

It was at that minute that the army of vendors descended on the man. They grabbed his gun first and threw him to the ground. Men grabbed each arm and each leg. A wily old woman unzipped his pants and grabbed his fifth appendage while holding a large knife for carving coconuts. Bria stepped closer.

"Why are you looking for Papà?" Bria demanded as she stood over the man. Several of the vendors ran for stones and tools.

"Don't fuck with me, Brianna," raged the man. He stared at the woman holding his penis and she grinned a dark, toothless grin. Bria smiled at her adoringly. As Devon stepped back from the bonded man, he watched Bria stand over him, demanding answers. He watched those who once feared her now ready to kill for her. He watched Bria control the situation with one simple nod and the words he would learn to dread.

"Ricorda il mio cognome." Remember my family's name.

Devon would never forget her name.

Devon and Bria watched the vendors beat her attacker with stones and hammers at Bria's command. The family was getting bigger.

Bria suddenly fell to the ground. "My father's alive?"

The End

READING GROUP GUIDE

1. The title of this book is BEACHSIDE MAFIA. Do you think this accurately reflects the novel? Why or why not? How do you feel about the word "Mafia?"

2. Bria is clearly troubled in the first half of the novel. Did you perceive her character as strong or weak? What made you feel this way? Did your opinion shange as the story unfolded?

3. What would you do if you were in the situation that Bria was in after being robbed of her possessions?

4. Bria asks tells Antonio, "I'm working on a project with the beach vendors. I want to help them but I'm unsure of how to get them to accept my help. If my father was here, he would know what to do." What would you have done differently to get the attention of the vendors?

5. Bria is taken by the peahen/peacock relationship as well as the hawk's presence. Discuss that imagry and what it meant. Is the hawk a harbinger? Is Bria a peacock or a peahen?

6. She references "Chi di gallina nasce, convien che razzoli," an old Italian proverb that states children are born to be like their

parents. Antonio believes she is referencing the vendors and their children. Bria adores her father, and is of him, but is she like him?

7. Where is the line between good and evil as it pertains to Bria Brigante?

8. Do you believe Antonio is part of the families looking for the lost Brigante fortune? Who should Bria trust?

9. Is Devon making the right decision? What would you do if you were Dylan Lancaster?

10. Devon or Antonio?

Made in the USA
Middletown, DE
10 February 2024